Cornish

Prideaux

Ghost

Stories

Featuring the Pridias family of Cornwall

From the

11th-13th Century

A CIP catalogue record for this title is

available from the British Library.

ISBN 978-0-9954609-5-9

www.paganuspublishing.co.uk

First Published in 2017

Paganus Publishing

Ruthin

Denbighshire

Paganus Publishing

FOREWORD

Cornish Prideaux Ghost Stories is one of the books in the series of the Pridias/Prideaux family throughout the centuries. Other titles are **Collected Prideaux Ghost Stories, A Ghost Story, A Christmas Story, More Prideaux Ghost Stories, Further Prideaux Ghost Stories** and **Prideaux Ghost Stories**.

Blood of the Lyon Men features Paganus de Pridias, Lord of Pridias and the story covers the death of his father Richard and the means by which his mother, Jehanne and his wife Tristen, both pure Melusine women, discover his murderer.

The Pattern of One features Richard de Pridias and follows his dealings with Ordagar, the ruthless Prior of Tywardreath and the resulting tragedy which occurs.

The Bridge of Incidents features Baldwin de Pridias. His story is about the bridge he built at Ponts Mill and the unusual guardians of the hermitage and the Pridias lands.

The Hanged Man features Nicholas de Pridias and his family and the strange events which occur in the woods and the chapel one stormy day.

The Jousting Lords features Richard de Pridias and his twin brother Herden. The story takes us to France and the Tournament circuit there and then brings us back to Cornwall where there is a most unusual event.

The Priestess features another Richard de Pridias and his meetings with a magical Priestess and the interactions with his sons, who believe he may be suffering from senile decay.

I Am Rich features Geoffrey de Pridias who is trying to find the secret documents his dead father Richard, has left for him in a secret place. His determination not to let the documents fall into the wrong hands leads him to a terrifying meeting he did not expect.

CAST LIST

Richard de Pridias (1011 – 1051) married Jehanne Melusine (1020 –1115)

Their son:

Paganus de Pridias (1040 – 1200) married Tristen Melusanne (1048 – 1150)

Their sons:

Philip de Pridias (1070 – 1079)

Richard de Pridias (1070 - 1122) married Morwenna (1099 – 1142)

Richard's son:

Baldwin de Pridias (1109 - 1165) married Gwen (1115 – 1135)

Their son:

Nicholas de Pridias (1135 - 1200) married Alana Cardinham (1140 – 1211)

Their sons:

Herden Hickadon de Pridias (1160 – 1197)

Richard de Pridias (1160 - 1225) married Guinevere (1165 – 1216)

Their son:

Richard de Pridias (1180 - 1250) married Morgana
(1180 – 1228)

Their sons:

Baldwin de Pridias (1196 – 1269)

Reginald de Pridias (1198 – 1273)

Geoffrey de Pridias (1200-1270) married Isabella
Orcherton (1206 – 1249)

Then married Nicholaa de la Kage (1229 – 1253)

Geoffrey and Isabella had two sons

Roger de Pridyas (1224 – 1291)

Piers de Pridyas (1229 – 1283)

CONTENTS

BLOOD OF THE LYON MEN

Featuring Paganus de Pridias, Lord of Pridias (1040 – 1100)

Every time Pagan rode back to his clifftop home, his mood would rise and fall in equal measure. He loved his land - every rock, meadow, tree and stream on it, but recently he returned to it more slowly.

His mother had told him that he should marry and continue their blood line and she had decided that Ethel of Fowey, daughter of Gaston Polred, was the ideal match. Ethel was a pretty girl and had a decent figure but she did not ride nor use a bow and she hated Nos, his constant companion.

Pagan shouted to Nos and he ran back to his master and continued to lope alongside the horse.

"Don't get too far ahead of us Nos, there are hunters who will take you to your next life earlier than you plan. And I cannot do without you."

Nos looked up at his companion, tongue lolling and tail relaxed and moved in a comfortable step as they crossed the moor. Pagan had just spent the past few days at Zennor negotiating a deal for some of the crystals which were plentiful on Pridias land. Most had to be dug for but recently some of the crystals were becoming visible at the cliff front. Pagan sent women to collect any they found on the beach when the tide receded and children were sent to collect any crystals they found higher up the cliff.

"I hear that gold has been found on your land too," said Alain de Prous during the negotiations. "And I want in."

Pagan had laughed at that and drunk more mead, knowing that Alain had a band of men who would be more than willing to fetch the gold themselves, defended or not by the Pridias clan.

"There has been gossip about that on other land too. The Saxon bastards were always interested and never found anything on their many raids through my lands."

"We have new masters now," said Alain.

"They are not my masters," snapped Pagan.

"And we'll give them the same welcome we gave Cola and his mates," chuckled Alain.

Pagan finished his drink and asked,

"That will be easy enough and I can count on you?"

"Always. After what those bastards did to your father, you can always count on us. Your mother has done a good job of raising you."

"She is your sister, the blood is right, isn't it?"

"Yes, and that is another subject I want to discuss."

Pagan looked up, curious.

"What?"

"I have a niece, your mother's niece too, who has been living over the water since she was a girl."

"Ireland?"

"No France, Normandy to be exact. She has been living in a convent there. She is now come of age and in need of a husband."

"And you want me to suggest someone?" Pagan was feeling that this discussion was going to end with him having to agree to something he would later regret.

"No lad, you know what I mean. You are to marry the girl and then we shall be joined officially and we both will have a reason to work together."

"No! Mother wants me to marry the Fowey girl because that family has helped us since Richard's death and if I come back with any other arrangement, we shall be at war with them and they live nearer to my land than you do."

"You told me yourself you don't want to marry her! You have nothing in common except for being neighbours."

"And your girl is better? What's her name?"

"Tristen, your mother knows of her although she has never met her. She was born in Cornwall and moved to Normandy when she was one. Her father had been killed in a similar way to Richard and so her mother took her to safety."

"Whereas my mother stayed on our land and taught me how to defend it and keep it. There was no way that she was letting those idiots take control. We Pridias have had control since before that Christ fellow they keep forcing upon us, was born."

"It's the same for all of us. We own the land and every invader wants to steal it or sell it when they leave. It's not theirs, it's ours."

"And their beliefs are not ours," agreed Pagan.

"No. This Jesus may have been a good man but I don't see why we have to leave our old ways behind."

"It's only control. Once Rome could no longer afford an army here, they decided to have the Church hold our eternity in their hands and it's all bollocks."

"You don't believe that God holds your destiny in his hands then?"

"No! I believe I hold my own destiny. What happens to me is my own decision and no one else's."

"You would get on very well with Tristen. She was put into that convent when she was young and she wants to leave before they do the whole head shaving and committing to marriage to Jesus and all that crap."

"So, you want me to save her?"

"Yes, and I want you to save her blood. Her line comes directly from Melusine like Jehanne and me, but Tristen's blood is purer as it comes through both her parents."

"There seems to be only a few Melusine descendants in the world. Not all of them want to breed I heard."

"Tristen wants a life and children."

"Not a husband?"

"I don't think a husband is high on her agenda, but she must have one if she wants any sort of life."

"Marry her to one of your sons then!"

"No. I have valuable contracts from them already. I want you to marry her and then we can trade and I will fight with you. I shall write to your mother and she will agree. She owes me."

Jehanne probably did owe Alain a lot. After the death of her husband, she and the ten-year-old Pagan would have lost all the estates without assistance. The favours she accepted had long arms and marrying Pagan to Ethel was repaying one of those favours.

Alain and Pagan embraced and he set off home, accompanied by Nos and Ddu, the black horse he had bought from a merchant when he docked at Fowey a year ago. The promised boat load of more Spanish horses had failed to arrive but Pagan remained hopeful. Pagan rode across the moor southwards and tracked through the wood until he reached the northern edge of his lands.

The family had been Lords here since part of the clan moved from flooded Lyonesse to the cousin ruled lands near Fowey. The Pridias Lords had originally taken their name from the southern edges of their lands – the clay cliffs. The meadows and woodland on the estate was intermittently broken by crags and streams and marsh and ended with the old hillfort caped with trees and rocks. The old wooden stockade compound had been replaced with a huge stone wall surrounding an inner village and Pridias Hall. This afforded them a view to the sea and the bay which culminated at Ponts Mill, their own harbour.

As he rode across the crags, Pagan began to remember the time he wanted to forget. The day that the men had come on their horses with their torches and their swords.

"Run to your mother Pagan," his father had shouted. And run he did, to the hidden beach where he knew his mother would be swimming and he could shut out the noises of the fighting and shouting and the terrible screaming. When he told his mother what was happening, she hid him in a cave safe from the high tide and said she would be back as soon as she could. Then she ran up the rocks to the cliff top and was out of sight. Pagan could hear noises of frightened people and clashing swords but saw no one until the following morning when his mother returned to him and she seemed to have aged 10 years.

Richard de Pridias had been stabbed, beheaded and left against the stone stockade sides along with several of his men and some of the women and children. The raiding party had come to steal horses and the gold they believed the Pridias family had. They only got as far as they did because the invaders usually soldiered for the local Saxon trouble causers and they were not ordinarily challenged or crossed. By the time Richard realised that their aims were murderous, it was too late. The Pridias fought well but were swiftly overcome, a penalty of not being battle ready.

When Jehanne Melusine de Pridias came running into the battle, her family were all but overpowered.

She picked up her dead husband's sword and swung it above her head before almost cutting the man she believed to be his executioner, in half. The man screamed and begged her for the death stroke but she only laughed and walked away before killing two more attackers. Jehanne screamed instructions at her people and soon the remaining bandits, including their leader, were cantering away, taking less with them than they had brought.

Jehanne called some of her own men as she mounted Richard's horse and they followed the raiders. Others from their village took care of the injured and two were instructed to row across the bay and fetch help. They were then to ferry back with help, for it was too far to ride inland to the bridge and ride back downriver. Jehanne had her bow and skilfully used it alongside her men, killing four escapees before they reached the Pridias boundary. Jehanne ordered that their bodies be dragged to the edge of the wood where she said the wolves would get rid of them. The only person to escape was the hooded leader whom Jehanne later learned was the real executioner and apparently, no one knew his identity, or was saying.

Following this terrible event with the support of her family and neighbours, she brought up her son as the Lord of the Pridias lands and taught him everything she knew, which was considerable. She brought in tutors only when necessary. Pagan loved her, respected her and feared her. Jehanne's familial line was as formidable as his, if not more so and everyone knew her skills. This was the woman that Pagan was now to tell about Alain's proposal.

Jehanne knew they needed support, but she would not want to alienate her neighbours.

When he walked inside the great hall, he saw his mother standing on the balcony looking out across the bay to Tywardreath. He walked and stood by her side. Nos pushed his head under her hand, forcing her to stroke him.

"How did it go?" she asked.

"He will help us and trade with us but on one condition."

"There is always a condition with Alain. What is it this time?"

Pagan looked at his mother. Her blonde-red hair was silhouetted against the setting sun. It hung long and straight to her waist allowing it freedom, while most other women covered theirs with a wimple. She wore her overdress of black and gold long over the underskirt, in a style contrary to her contemporaries. Although in a vow of perpetual mourning for her husband, she nevertheless wore jewellery about her person and her hair, the jangling of which would announce her arrival.

"The other women will soon follow my fashion," she said to her maid, Gertrude.

Whether they would or not, Jehanne was more beautiful at 50 than many women half her age. Men admired her and women envied her. She was a goddess the like of whom Pagan wanted as a wife and they both knew that the Fowey girl was not up to scratch.

"He wants me to marry some cousin of mine who doesn't like living in a Normandy convent."

He was surprised when Jehanne grabbed his arm and asked, "Who?"

"Some girl called Tristen."

Jehanne put her hand to the pendant dangling among her many neck decorations.

"I thought she was dead."

"Not very dead Mother. I told him I could not marry because you have promised me to the delightful Ethel."

"I can soon get you out of that," she said.

This was an unexpected reaction, Pagan had expected anger and refusal.

"You go and bathe my son, you stink after your journey and I shall ride to Polred and meet with Gaston. If Tristen is still alive, then you shall marry her and keep our line pure."

Nos went to follow her and Pagan called him back. Jehanne had wolves of her own, all of which were related to Nos. The de Pridias family believed in purity of blood, whether within their own clan or with their animals.

She held her hand up as she walked away, signalling no more talk and hitched up her skirts as she ran down the wooden stairs to the ground. Pagan watched her pull herself on to her horse and ride away, accompanied by two guards. He crossed from the balcony to the edge of the wall and saw them gallop away from the cliffs and beach towards the bridge, two miles upstream which they would have to cross in order to ride back towards Tywardreath and beyond.

Gaston Polred had the lands down to the wood-covered headland. The property was divided by a small river that culminated in a pool stained red by the minerals and ore it ran through. Gaston had helped her a great deal following Richard's death and had asked her to marry him several times. His own wife died two months after Richard, after a fall from the cliffs at the headland. Some said that Gaston had been involved in the raid and wanted Jehanne and her lands. While Pagan was too young to take control, there was plenty of gossip about what could happen in the years between an heir being ten years old and his coming of age.

As it turned out, Jehanne was more than capable of running the show and kept Pagan close and her people loyal and so needed no husband. The same gossips believed that getting Pagan to marry Ethel was the next best thing for Gaston Polred.

Jehanne was an excellent rider and they arrived quickly at Polred Hall.

"My dear Jehanne, I am so pleased to see you!"

Gaston embraced her warmly and beckoned the priest who was with him to leave them alone. The man bowed and walked to the side of the hall.

"In need of spiritual guidance Gaston?"

"No, my conscience is clear. I was discussing the wedding plans, is that why you are here?"

"Yes. I have come to tell you that the marriage cannot go ahead as my son is promised to another."

"Since when? You cannot go back on this contract!" Gaston was instantly angry, a state his men were used to seeing but one he had never yet shown to

Jehanne. He could see his hopes of marriage and control over the lands across the bay slipping away.

"I would not go back on a contract Gaston, but I have only recently discovered that the girl Pagan was promised to when he was a child, is still alive."

"Has she been resurrected from the dead?"

"Something like that. We were told she was dead when she was eight, not long before my husband was murdered. She caught the plague in Normandy at her convent and apparently died. But I have heard only today that she survived and I cannot in all conscience proceed with the marriage between Pagan and Ethel. It would go against God."

Jehanne looked over to the priest for confirmation and he nodded his agreement. She thought Gaston was going to explode. He smashed the table with his fists and threw a bowl at her head,

"Gaston! Control yourself! This is no way for a civilised man to behave!"

Gaston lurched across the room and grabbed Jehanne by the throat. She put her own hands up to his in an attempt to remove them.

As they struggled, her many stranded necklaces broke and her gold symbols, one containing some of Richard's possessions, fell to the ground. Gaston did not stop his attack but Jehanne was now empowered and she ripped his arms from her neck. Then she struck him hard in the chest and he fell back against the tall candle sticks. The noise finally brought assistance in the shape of the priest and two of Gaston's servants who ran to lift their master while the priest came to the side of Jehanne.

"My Lady, are you hurt?"

"Only slightly Father but he has broken my necklaces which are very precious to me. Please help me collect them."

He picked up the chains and pendants and it was then that Ethel walked in to the room.

"So, I am not to be your daughter, Jehanne?"

"No, my dear. You will have to wed your Lystwithiel fellow now, Ethel. Not such a good breeding line but at least you won't be alone."

"Like you?" replied Ethel.

Jehanne walked over to the girl, slapped her hard and said,

"Don't cross me Ethel."

Jehanne left and rode back home, smiling.

*

Tristen Melusanne arrived at the Pridias home in a procession constituting twenty men and four women. Jehanne and Pagan watched her arrival from the walls. The double line of horses and their riders rode in front and behind the horse which held his bride-to-be. She was dressed in white and wore a veil and cloak which completely covered her face and form. It seemed that Pagan must wait before he could view the woman he had agreed to look after for the rest of her life.

As they neared the house, a drum beaten by one of her outriders echoed. A single beat in time with their horse-steps brought Pridias villagers out of their homes until, without instruction, they lined her route.

Pagan looked at his mother and saw that she was looking at the procession more intently than she had ever looked at anything. He hoped all this was going to work out. He had agreed to the marriage contract but had no intention to be constantly at the side of his new wife.

Pagan had been surprised at the change in his mother following her return from visiting Gaston. She seemed more determined and focused. Writing back to Alain she not only agreed to the marriage but demanded that Tristen was brought home from Normandy and immediately despatched to their estates. Jehanne would only say that it was imperative for the family to keep Tristen safe.

As the procession arrived at the gates they were opened by guards and the procession moved through in time to the drum. Just before Tristen rode under the archway she looked up and Pagan swore that she left her horse and brought her face into his. But he must have been mistaken for she soon vanished from sight under the gateway and now they must descend the stairs and welcome the group. Tristen did not speak, her maids instead asking about her quarters and giving a list of demands to which Jehanne readily agreed. Tristen floated behind her maids into the rooms allocated to her until the wedding could take place at the church dedicated to Saint Blaise at Landreath which lay southwards along the cliffs.

There was a tall stone cross near the site which the Saxon invaders had helped erect and carve. It had been there for almost one hundred and fifty years and lay just inside the wall encircling the Pridias village. It was considered magical by the villagers and was often decked with flowers and charms.

"When do I get to meet her?" asked Pagan.

"At the wedding tomorrow."

"She might look like a boar!"

"She won't. She's a Melusine like me. She will be clever and beautiful and skilled." Jehanne put her hand to the jewelled pendant box hanging at her breast and whispered, "Now we shall know. Finally."

Pagan knew that the only thing his mother wanted to know was who had killed his father and he wondered how Tristen would be able to help.

He forgot all about the problem by the time he stood at the cross waiting for his bride to arrive. Tristen arrived attired similarly to her arrival yesterday. Her dress and tunic were threaded with gold and jewels and her cape was made from a pale fur and bordered with gold. Tristen brought no money to the contract although Jehanne said she brought more than wealth. She said that his new wife assured their protection against the upcoming and apparently unavoidable land grab by the Norman invaders.

Pagan dictated the details of the days following the wedding to a young monk who often visited the area. It seemed that the Church was looking at establishing a monastery across the bay if the money could be raised. The monk was disturbed about some of the elements of Pagan's story but knowing that miracles happened often, dutifully transcribed the words in his excellent hand.

This is what was written.

Shortly after our wedding it was obvious that my mother Jehanne and my wife Tristen were more than aunt and niece. I have always been aware that Jehanne had abilities unusual to all but the most accomplished of sorcerers. Now I learnt that my wife had the same skills and together they decided to achieve two initial goals. Firstly, to discover the identity of the man who murdered my father and secondly, to save and secure the Pridias ancestral lands. Our lands have, from the beginning of man's memory been in our possession and they run the length of the cliffs to the south, down to the sea and beyond the river to the east to Golant, to the north we own parts of Lanlivery and Luxulyan and beyond to the feet of the moor and to the west we own Stenalees and beyond. We own lands at St Breock and St Issey and beyond to the north coast. Our Hall is perched at the cliff edge at the bay and has a perfect view of the sea. This William man who has incorrectly termed himself King, has no rights over our Celtic and Kernewek lands.

My father Richard de Pridias had been killed and beheaded when a raiding party came to our home. My mother Jehanne and some of our fighting men saw off and killed most of the men, but were told that the man who stabbed and removed the head of the popular leader of their lands had escaped. No one had recognised him because he wore a leather hood but it had been reported that before he took the final deadly blow he removed it.

Jehanne had supervised the burial of Richard and only told me years later that she had removed my father's eyes. I was shocked to hear this news. I believed to that point that the box pendant Jehanne wore all the time contained only Richard's hair. Jehanne had always told me that she carried my father with her wherever she went but had failed to mention that it was his eyes.

I refrained from asking how she removed his eyes as I did not wish to know. Even though we live in such violent times, I have killed no one whereas I know of twelve men killed by Jehanne. She was not so weak as me in this regard.

We are told that the final sight of a person before they die is reflected in their eyes and the last thing Richard saw was his murderer. Jehanne said that she would wait until she was able to view the reflection. The eyes were kept in separate airtight compartments in the gold box, so that one could be removed without tainting the other.

At Pridias we have a building further along the coast which is used for meditation and worship. There is a central table with candles, bowls and a gold crucifix. On the circular walls are hundreds of candles on three layers of shelves, some of which are always lit. All the candles are lit when it is very cold or when there are special ceremonies. We celebrate our own beliefs in addition to the enforced Roman Christianity, ignorance of which would mean great trouble for us if commented upon by our neighbours to the self-righteous Bishops.

It was here that Jehanne tried her first experiment with my help. At almost midnight on the night of the

Winter Solstice, all the candles were lit. The door was locked and instructions had been given that we to be disturbed under no account. Jehanne placed a silver mirror on the altar and Richard's left eye was placed on a raised gold plate in front of it. Behind that and in direct line with the mirror and eye was another plate containing some minerals which Jehanne said she had bought from a sea merchant at great expense quite recently. She spoke out aloud to my father's spirit and asked that he help us in our task.

The mineral was lit and it shot a hot bright light through the eye and it was there! A milky white image on the glass of a man and even the sword shape was visible. We held our breath as the image began to clear and then as a strange wind circulated the room, the mineral spluttered and stopped and the image faded.

It was over and we were none the wiser. Richard's eye was decaying before us and we both knew that our chance had passed. I had not known that Jehanne had asked Tristen to bring more mineral with her from France where merchants could obtain it more easily from the Arabian countries. The Melusine women would be able to work better together she told me.

Meantime, I supervised our farming and hunting and ensured the building work was done and soldiers trained and the fishermen had their nets ready. I spoke to visiting monks and saints and allowed hermits to travel through our lands and stay and rest in return for prayers and medicinal skills. I organised the mining and sale of the crystals and through only a few trusted men – gold.

Jehanne and Tristen would talk often and meet in our own chapel and discuss – I didn't know what. Then one day I was told that they were ready for the second and final experiment. I was also informed that I was to be present at this momentous occasion which was destined to succeed. This time it took place on the Summer solstice and with a full moon, it almost was not dark enough at midnight. By the time we shut the chapel door and lit all the candles the atmosphere was set fair and we were sure we would get a result. I never stopped to think what we would do when we saw the image. Jehanne said, "I will avenge your father Pagan, it is not of your concern."

We followed the same process as before and even I was aware that Tristen added energy to the proceedings. This time when the minerals were lit there was enough light to last almost a minute and there, reflected on the mirror was a face we recognised immediately.

It was Gaston Polred.

It took the three of us one hour to reach the stone and wooden home of our supposedly good neighbour Gaston. The Saxon, Cola had once been in overall governance of Polred lands but now that the Normans were taking control in England it was only a matter of time before he would have a new master. That night none of us were interested in outcomes as we were set only for revenge. Tristen was as determined as anyone who had known him personally. Jehanne was correct, there could never have been anyone other than Tristen for me.

A servant peered through the small hatch in the main door of the Polred Hall revealing only his dirty hood and grizzled face. He told us that his master was not at home. I told him I did not believe him and would kill him if he did not open the door. He said if I threatened him again he would send out fighting men and I informed him that I would kill them one by one and we argued in this childish manner until Jehanne stopped us. She asked where Polred was and the servant said he had ridden along the cliff tops and then down through the woods towards the headland at the edge of the bay.

We mounted again and rode down the coast track, feeling the sea spray from the high tide as the increasing wind threw it in our direction. We did not speak when the sun began to rise at our backs and brought into view a scruffy looking man on his horse. As we approached, he turned around and then dismounted.

By the time we were in front of him, Gaston shook and whimpered and said. "I am sorry Richard. I wanted your lands and your family and your life and tried to get it. I was wrong and will be punished for it. You have come to collect me and I am ready."

We looked to our right flank and out of the rays of the rising sun, rode my father in the same black and gold tunic which has always represented the Pridias family. Jehanne moved her horse towards his horse and Richard raised his hand to stop her and she understood. He patted his sword, the same sword I now carried and smiled. To Tristen he bowed and then he rode towards Gaston. Richard suddenly kicked his horse to a gallop and Gaston turned to run away and in so doing he ran straight over the cliffs. Richard continued to ride over the cliff and did not *fall. As the sun came completely over the hills and bay to our rear, Richard and his horse vanished.*

Gaston's servant and three armed men rode up behind us and then towards the cliff edge. "I saw Richard de Pridias chase him over the cliff," said one.

"His spirit did," said another.

This is exactly what happened and I want it to be on record for future generations to take note. The next time my father was seen was at my mother's deathbed many years afterwards. This is a true account

Paganus de Pridias

Lord of Pridias.

THE PATTERN OF ONE

Featuring Richard de Pridias

(1170-1122)

Richard de Pridias was sitting on the beach at the base of the cliffs watching his wife Morwenna and his son Baldwin play in the water. They were trying to teach him to swim but Baldwin had no aptitude, instead preferring to play with the wolves. Richard a non-swimmer himself, had empathy with the boy.

It was a perfect sunny day and the sea was calm. He could see boats ferrying men across to Tywardreath and coming in from the bay with fish and crabs. The larger merchant and fishing boats crossed the end of the bay on their way to Fowey and back. Some ships travelled eastwards to other Cornish ports and across the Channel to the Normandy coast. The seabirds swooped against the cloudless sky and down to the water, hopeful that some of the food the family ate might go their way. Sadly for them, crumbs went into the mouths of the wolves and any attempt to steal was met with dangerous snaps and growls.

Richard stood up and brushed the sand from his leather tunic, the action encouraging Nosbach to run to his master and push his hand onto his own muzzle.

"Come on boy, we have to work."

"Can't you stay longer?" asked his wife.

"No. Tristen wants me to look at some documents about the Priory. They are intent on finishing it apparently."

Subconsciously they looked across their bay to the church perched a little back from the Tywardreath pier. To the seaward side was a tall wooden scaffolding tower covering the consecrated stones supposed to be used when the initial building blocks were laid in 1088. The building had been inconsistent, sometimes money ran out or was suddenly withdrawn and the local workmen starved or feasted or went back to sea, per the current state of play. Deaths of authority figures, both pastoral and legal and arguments over land and rights had delayed the project and 34 years on they were only partway through the build and still arguing. Now Richard was to attend a meeting with the delegated and ruthless Canon Ordagar and sign a treaty promising fighting men and money and land. If he didn't, they would be under yet another threat to have their own land taken from them. His late father Pagan had fought tooth and claw to keep the Pridias lands and Tristen his widow, had cast her spells. These incantations were performed in the early days with her mother-in-law Jehanne and following her death, alone. So far, the incantations had been very effective.

Richard kissed his wife and son, patted his leg summoning Nosbach and ran up the cliff. Richard hadn't ridden down, preferring to walk through the meadows to the beach. Even as he moved away from the beach towards Pridias Hall he could not help looking back at the sea. He could never tire of living here.

The grass, sandwort, orache and purslane and sedge quickly gave way to yarrow, lady's bedstraw and mint. He knew that a little further upriver he would find flag iris in yellow, blue and white, marsh marigolds and mallows. As he neared the edge of the tree line, the wood sorrel, woodruff, garlic and sweet nettles let out their heady scents. The trees, oak, beech, ash and alder hid the birds, squirrels and further inland at the dark centre of the wood the wolf families, boars and deer roamed.

He could never risk losing these ancestral Pridias lands to the Norman carpetbaggers who now enforced their self-serving laws. He must do what his family had always done, playact subservience and proact rebellion.

His mother waved at him from the wall and he fondly remembered his Nain Jehanne doing the same thing before her death seven years prior. Jehanne had been put to rest alongside Pagan and Taid Richard so carefully by Tristen and two of their local hermits. Jehanne rested in her specially designed coffin in a blue and silver threaded gown. Her pale red hair had been braided elegantly with gold and crystals and laid over her arms which were crossed over her breast. Unlike so many women, neither Jehanne nor Tristen needed to braid the hair of donor women into their own in order to make it look thicker and longer. Some women even added long silver cups and tassels at the hair ends to achieve the same effect. There had been discussion from others that Jehanne's dead arms should be held in prayer over her breast, but that idea was swiftly vetoed. Jehanne believed in her own power and would not bow to an outside idol, perhaps interpreting the Bible teachings rather better than the Bishops had.

Tristen met him as he walked through the gate and they made their way over to the chapel. Richard swung the heavy door open and they both entered before closing it firmly and bringing across the oak bar.

"I cannot wait long Tristen, I have to meet at Tywardreath and go through the convention for the future of our lands."

"I know my son. You must not panic, we shall retain them and secure our future."

"Spells and potions?"

"I trust that you are not joking Richard. Keep your focus on how you want your life to play out."

Richard said nothing, he was aware of how it worked and knew that he must never imagine anything he did not want to happen. He wanted to tell his mother about the feelings of impending doom he had hanging over him. She would tell him to change his thoughts and lately he was finding that advice irritating.

"I am, Mother. Now, what do you want me here for?"

"Seven years."

"I don't understand."

"It is seven years since Jehanne passed. It is time to collect her bones and relics."

"I'm not doing any of that," Richard said with a harshness in his voice that he had not intended to convey.

"You won't have to. I will do it and Geraint and Myfor will help me. There will be nothing gooey left on her bones, you know that's why we wait seven years."

"I know Tristen, it just seems a bit...like witchcraft."

Tristen caught his arm with a strength that defied her 74 years. She looked like a 30-year-old and he thought of Jehanne and the day she died at 95 years old. She had spent the day at the beach, walked back and gone into the chapel. She was a very fit and young looking – supposedly, old lady. Tristen had found her when Jehanne failed to return for her evening meal and she soon went about her Melusine business on Jehanne's body. The funeral had been a splendid affair.

Geraint and Myfor were two of her assistant monks whom she was teaching herbal medicine in return for their regular prayers for the more religious Pridias villagers. The rattle on the chapel door soon revealed their arrival for the task.

"I am going, Tristen."

"Where is the meeting?"

"Polred Hall. I am to meet Ordagar the Canon and the Polreds are supplying a place to meet."

Tristen looked up and said, "Beware that slimy weasel Ordagar and the Polreds. They are still holding a grudge. Here..."

Tristen took a pendant from her neck. "Wear this around your neck. It will keep you safe."

He took it and walked outside, putting the pendant into a tunic pocket. He had no intention of arriving with a feminine necklace to such an important meeting.

His escape was stopped by his mother shouting from the chapel door.

"Wait Richard, I want you to take a letter to the Canon."

*

He handed the letter to Ordagar as soon as he was shown into Polred Hall.

"Thank you, I always like to hear from the Lady Tristen. She is a special person."

"Yes sir. I think so."

"She has managed very well since your father passed to his higher reward."

"Yes, she has accepted that your God saw fit to send that storm while he was out on a previously calm sea."

"My God?"

"I suspect he is more yours than mine sir."

"Perhaps, perhaps."

Ordagar poured Richard a drink and then pulled a chair away from the table and untied the parchment.

He read it carefully and read it again and rolled it back up and retied it.

"Do you know what it says?" he asked.

"No sir, I have no idea."

"Then I shall not tell you but please tell her yes, I shall be honoured to accept. Now, let us discuss your rights to the lands across the bay."

"I like to think that we are entitled to the lands. The Pridias family have lived here since before Lyonesse fell, and hundreds of years before that."

"You are related to King Mark?"

"And by definition Tristan and Iseult? I heard you have been searching for their meeting place."

"An interest of mine I'm afraid."

"They met at Golant, by the church there. And King Mark was based at the hill fort over there," Richard pointed to the north east. "At Castle Dor."

"I have heard that. Perhaps you can give me a tour one
day?"

"Certainly. There are some very interesting places on Pridias land too," said Richard, spotting an advantage.

"Hmmm. And you think it would be a shame to let the land fall into the hands of a Norman?"

"I do."

Ordagar handed him a roll of parchment,

"I don't read this fancy Latin script," said Richard, handing it back.

"By all means, I can tell you what it says."

Ordagar walked over to the window and began,

"One Knights fee in the manor of Pidias, to hold to Richard de Pidias and his heirs, except an acre of land in Carnubelbanathel for which the monks of Tywardreath rendered annually to the said Richard 20d for all customs, &cc, as written in this charter of convention between Ordagar the Canon and Richard de Pidias."

"It's Pridias."

"I will have it altered. Do you agree to the terms?"

"Do I have any choice?"

"My Lord FitzTorold will take all the lands if you argue. This way you get to keep everything and from what I see here there is a substantial acreage and perhaps it is worth bowing to another to keep it."

"And Carnubelbanathel?"

"If you let the monks continue to use it, that helps your case. I certainly have put forward the argument."

"Thank you. I don't expect that Polred is happy about this?"

"He doesn't know yet. He also doesn't know that he will be losing control over most of his own land to the Crown. He won't be happy."

"May I ask why you have been so helpful to our family?"

Ordagar laughed.

"The Melusine blood has influence in more places than you could possibly know."

Richard nodded,

"With a Melusine Nain and Mother I have seen plenty, don't you worry."

"I would like to hear about it. As you know..."

"It is an interest of yours."

"Yes, and a good job for you that it is."

"I am sorry sir. I did not mean to sound rude. What did my mother tell you?"

"Now that is where I must plead privacy. Ask your mother."

When Richard left Polred Hall and the young servant girl had smiled at him as she let him out of the door, he decided to ride over to the Priory site. There were a few workmen around but they were only half-heartedly dressing stones and erecting stockade fencing. The wooden scaffold surrounding the area where the tower was to be looked as though it would have to be rebuilt before any more serious work was to be done. The Priory was not half-finished and there didn't seem an intention that it would begin soon. Richard expected that his demanded financial contribution in return for his land would help.

Richard looked out to sea where ships sailed against the clear blue sky. He had to put his hand to his eyes against the bright sun which was gradually slipping down to the horizon. He looked back to the bay where he could see his Hall atop the old fort and the woods which caped the seaward side and the meadows which stopped at the clay cliff and the beach below. The tide was going out and that meant only the ferry and the smaller boats were using the water. Further up river and miles out of sight, was the bridge everyone used to circumnavigate the bay but near Ponts Mill, there was a lower causeway which could be crossed at the lowest tide. Here the traveller must be very quick and have a certain knowledge of the tide times.

His horse was becoming restless and as he bent to stroke him Richard heard howling. He saw Nosbach at the clifftop on the other side of the bay and the wolf had seen him. The wolf jumped down onto the beach and began splashing in the water. He started to wade in and Richard shouted out to him to stop but Nosbach couldn't hear him. The wolf began to swim and Richard didn't know what to do for the best. Shouting would only encourage him and if he rode back to the bridge, Nosbach may panic. He should have brought him to the meeting. They usually went everywhere together.

Then he saw Tristen running down the meadow to the cliff edge and Nosbach turned his head, hesitated and then began swimming back to the beach. Tristen waved to Richard and all was well again.

"Your mother is a clever lady," said a voice behind which revealed itself to belong to Ordagar.

"I thought he was going to drown."

"You love your wolf?"

"I do sir. We have a few at home."

"I always wanted a wolf."

"They take a lot of looking after and like to roam free."

"Yes, and I am always wandering around the country. I have to go to the north coast later this week."

"It is better that a wolf stays in his own hunting ground even when he has a master. They cannot be chained anywhere."

"I am sure. Tell your mother I will be back in seven days and we can do the thing she suggested then."

Richard smiled and kicked his horse on. The workmen nodded to him and Richard cantered through the village towards the bridge. The people looked at him with envy or scorn depending upon their own view of Lords and their lands.

Richard eased his horse as he arrived at the causeway. It was quicker to go home this way and he was worried about Nosbach. The water was now low enough and as it was a receding tide it could only get drier. It would save him almost an hour on his trip and he was sorely tempted to try it. He saw Nosbach and Tristen standing on the bank opposite and she waved. Nosbach was edging forward.

"Come on boy, lets risk it."

His horse twirled and spun and refused to move ahead. Richard kicked him and squeezed his legs, forcing him forward. The horse put one hoof on to the sand but as soon as he felt it sink a little, he reared and pulled back. Richard was not a cruel man and decided not to frighten the animal unnecessarily and so dismounted. A boy he knew came to him and Richard hailed him.

"Can you ride, boy?"

"Sir - yes my Lord."

"Do you know who I am?"

"You are the Lord of the Pridias sir."

"I am and you are the son of Philip the smith at Tywardreath."

"I am, sir."

"Take my horse back to the bridge and bring him to my Hall. You will be paid and I shall send you back on the ferry. No need to guide him, just hold on. He will know the way, so no ideas about gadding off on a longer ride."

"Right sir. You can rely on me sir. My Lord, are you sure about crossing here?"

"Of course, don't you worry."

"Only it seems a bit..."

"Get going boy."

The boy jumped easily on to the horse who accepted him without trouble.

"My Lord, I would like to come and work for you and take care of the horses or something like that. There is no work for me here and I do like wolves too."

Richard looked up at the raggedly-dressed boy sitting on his beautifully turned out stallion and said,

"See how you get on with him. We will talk when you bring him to me safely."

"I promise, my Lord."

Richard patted his horse and the boy turned him upstream. He heard a noise from the opposite bank and saw Nosbach standing on the far end of the causeway. The wolf had no fear of the receding water. Tristen waved again and stood behind the wolf. Richard walked forward and felt his boots sink into the sand and he withdrew them immediately. He had imagined it would be drier but when Nosbach began to bark Richard couldn't resist the urge to cross. He walked purposefully towards his mother and wolf and tried to ignore his wet legs and tunic. He also chose to ignore the shouts from the Tywardreath bank because he couldn't see what that was about.

It was several seconds before he realised that he was struggling to keep afloat and the weight of water on his tunic and sword was pulling him under. He was choking and spluttering and in his confusion felt his mind racing between panic and disbelief. There had been no water and it was a receding tide. It was not possible that the water was now above his head.

"Tristen!" he shouted. "Nosbach, help me!"

Richard was trying to keep the panic out of his voice as he splashed and struggled and his mouth went under again. Nosbach was at his side and Richard grabbed for him but couldn't reach. He saw Tristen on the bank and shouted, "Mother! I need help!"

He heard more shouting and some screaming and a little voice shouting, "Father! Shall I fetch the boat?" It was Baldwin and Richard couldn't bear that his son would see him drown.

"Baldwin! Go back to the Hall!" But his words could not be heard as his head was under the water. He felt a slight urge to cough and then it was over.

He was on the Pridias bank with Nosbach licking his face and Tristen standing over him.

"Is Baldwin alright?" he asked.

"Baldwin will be fine. He is a good boy and will make a good man."

"Hello my son. We weren't expecting you just yet."

It was Pagan and the woman was not Tristen, but Jehanne.

"I am dead?"

"Drowned, Richard, like me."

"You only swopped one time for another. Nothing to fear here. See? We have the lands and the sea and not one thieving Norman or Saxon or Polred can take it from us."

Richard sat up and looked around. Pridias looked the same and there was the sea and his parents and a man who looked remarkably like Pagan.

"Why? Why have I drowned? I have just secured the lands!"

"Ordagar is a liar and a poisoner and wants Pridias," said Jehanne.

"He will fail however. Baldwin will keep the lands. Tristen will see to that."

"I saw Tristen and Nosbach on the bank," said Richard.

"You saw me and Nosbach drowned when he tried to swim over to you. He is here too, playing with Nos."

Richard fell back on to the bank, unable to take it in.

*

Morwenna hugged Baldwin to her breast and they both sobbed.

"Is Father dead? Like Nosbach?"

Morwenna continued to cry and Tristen put her arm around the both of them before returning to her son's body. She closed the eyes on his wet face and beckoned over her monks.

"Take him to the chapel," she instructed. "Ordagar did this."

"How do you know?" asked Gwyn, Richard's chief guard.

"Trust me Gwyn. I know and we shall have our revenge. Ordagar poisoned my son so that he hallucinated and he will die for it."

Richard was taken to the chapel and washed and dressed ready for his internment. Jehanne's dry bones were already washed and had been split into three gold urns.

"One for the Priory, one for our chapel and one... well I won't tell you where that has been kept until you are older, Baldwin. But be assured Jehanne will protect our lands and the family and their interests."

"I am the Lord Pridias now Nain Tristen, but I am not yet prepared."

"I will stay alive until you are ready, Baldwin. You will be as good a Lord as your father and all your fathers before. Richard shall be kept here alongside Pagan and Taid Richard."

"Where are my other Lord Pridias buried?"

"On the moor. They will rise when they are needed. But always know this Baldwin, a Pridias lives forever."

She hugged him tight and nodded across to Gwyn.

He would deal with Ordagar, however long it took. The letter would ensure that he found him.

THE BRIDGE OF INCIDENTS

Featuring Baldwin de Pridias

(1109 – 1165)

"Are they still arguing about that?"

"Yes, and I have again informed them of our position. The lands are ours and not Cardinham lands."

"I don't know how many times I need to tell them. More than I have already done it seems."

Baldwin was tired. He had been Lord Pridias for 34 years following the sad demise of his father Richard. During that time, he had agreed to help where he could with the now completed Priory at Tywardreath in return for the security of his own lands. Once the contract had been signed, he backed off from the deal, watering the commitment down in his own favour. He learned swiftly that once the local labourers and craftsmen had taken their wages for building the Priory, they had no desire to fund the monks in their judgements and lectures. They had their own hermits and experts in plants for medicine or poison and had no need of these self-righteous interlopers who came to save the Cornish lost souls.

Baldwin and his family would always side with their own people. Tywardreath Priory and their Benedictine 'black monks' would have to rely for the most part on handouts from their sister monastery in France.

He had also had a bridge built upriver from the sea moorings at Ponts Mill and the sea causeway where his father had drowned. Baldwin remembered the day he saw his father walk into the sea because he believed that the causeway was dry. He had watched him drown and then seen his lifeless body dragged to shore. Tristen, he thought of Nain so fondly even now, said that Ordagar had poisoned Richard and she had made him pay. Ordagar was soon dead too, a victim of unidentified armed villains on his way to the north coast. Osbert was the Prior currently and had initially taken up the role in 1130 while he supervised the last years of completion until 1135 when the Priory officially opened for business. Osbert had hoped for a constant influx of paying locals worshiping and asking for forgiveness, instead he had a queue of men demanding favourable treatment in whatever deal they had in mind.

Shortly afterwards King Stephen had established his murderous control of England and money and food soon became scarce. There were hundreds of starving and ruthless strangers roaming the lands and willing to kill for food. Any person rebelling against the King was tortured and executed horrendously in the castles Stephen began to build around the country, several of which were in Cornwall.

That was when Restormel Castle began its life at Lystwithiel and where many lost their lives. Baldwin had struggled to keep his people fed and his lands his own. He had ensured that his animals were kept safe and guarded from the starving vagabonds who roamed the countryside ready to kill whatever came into their path. These unwelcomes would steal, kill and eat horses, wolves and cats when cattle, sheep or poultry could not be found. These villains were either executed and buried in secret or thrown outside Pridias boundaries as a warning to others. Hungry Pridias inhabitants would be sent to the hermitage or the Hall for sustenance.

The hermitage was on the western side of the bridge that Baldwin had built. A portion of the alms from the hermitage and the use of the lands surrounding it, went directly to the Priory in return for assistance when necessary.

The bridge was stone and timber built and substantial enough for carts to cross. It was on the River Par, north of the sea harbour at Ponts Mill, to where small ships would sail and dock. It had been Pridias men and Pridias money that had built it, but the Cardinhams and the Turstins were trying to lay claim to it. King Stephen was now dead and he sought to gain support of the new masters. Baldwin Fitz Turstin was trying to use as proof that it was he who had built it on his own lands, because the bridge had come to be known as Baldwin's Bridge. He had used King Stephen – a personal friend, he insisted – as a threat and Baldwin de Pridias had told him what to do with his threats. Now, Fitz Turstin did not feel so secure.

It was Baldwin's nineteen-year-old son Nicholas who was currently informing him of the new claim to the bridge. Nicholas was born the same day the Priory had been declared complete and open for business and he was considered locally as a 'special child'. Why that should be so when his mother had died during his birth condemning Baldwin to a celibate life, had confused them both.

Jehanne, Tristen, Morwenna and Gwen were all dead and there were no Pridias daughters. Soon it would be time to find Nicholas a wife and perhaps he would produce more children than the family had managed to date.

"Is Turstin still backing him?" asked Baldwin.

"Yes. They are making a push before the new King has a clean sweep and the past twenty years are put behind us. I expect they want to make a final claim to the bridge and hermitage and I am not allowing it to happen."

"Neither am I, son."

The bridge was a useful trade route as prior to its construction, travellers had to go much further inland or use the causeway or ferry across the bay. Now travellers paid a toll to an armed guard or two and part of this toll was given in alms to the hermitage. Other travellers wanted to call at the hermitage to visit with the resident sage who had more than likely come from Ireland to Padstow and then across the moor. There had always been a friendly welcome at Pridias from before remembered time. Now this little chapel gave them a place to stay and meditate and heal. The hermit collected their monies and the Priory had their portion. The Priory would sometimes send a monk of their own in order to make sure that nothing happened there which was against God or the King Stephen.

"Alright Nicholas. It will be fine. Now, there is something I think you should know."

"Not another family secret, Baldwin!"

Nicolas pulled a chair from the table and sat down. He accepted the offered wine from his father and smiled. Throughout his formative years, he had learned of the skills of his Mother and Nain. He knew of the wolves and their almost psychic abilities. He knew about the mysterious death of Gaston Polred and many healing miracles. Nicholas knew that he must not talk about any story which resembled witchcraft or event which could not be ascribed to God. Spies were everywhere and the perpetrator was soon reported, dragged off to a secure place by armed men and tortured until he came up with some random names and then he was still executed in a terrible way.

"Another secret Nicholas, you need to know all of the Pridias secrets to pass on to your son when you marry."

"I hope you are not yet contracting a wife for me?"

"No. But as you are the only Pridias blood after me, you must waste no time."

"Not very prolific, are we?"

"Not in this world, no."

"So, tell me."

"The bridge, you remember why I built it?"

"Because of Richard drowning and I know he was poisoned by the lying, thieving Canon. He too is dead and I am glad about that," answered Nicholas.

"Yes, because of my father and because of trade, the income from which has helped us and the Priory."

"And subsequently kept our property safe from all idiots."

"Indeed. But there is much more to it than that. Tristen summoned something to protect us and the bridge before she went. She helped as much as she could, even after your mother died. Sadly, she could not stay with us forever and so she left us a permanent guardian who cannot be paid, swayed, killed or removed. The guardian is ours forever and has protected us and our lands so far. These Cardinhams and Turstins cannot take any of our properties or people while the guardian exists."

"I have seen no guardian. Is he one of our men? Or a Melusine witch I don't yet know?"

"We both have Melusine blood, do not mock. The guardian lives at the hermitage by the bridge," chided Baldwin.

"One of those saints?"

"The guardian is no saint. In the wrong hands, he is the exact opposite of a saint."

"I am intrigued Father. May I meet him?"

"Tonight there is a lunar eclipse. We can only see him during an eclipse. So tonight, I will show you."

"It will be the third lunar eclipse this year, so they aren't that rare."

"I didn't say they were rare, just that is the only time we can see him."

Nicholas smiled, he loved his father but still felt the need to remind him of how clever his son was.

"In fact, there was a lunar eclipse on the first day of this year!" added Nicholas.

"One more word about lunar eclipses and I will eclipse you round the head," said Baldwin.

They both laughed, their close bond since Gwen died had matured and remained as Nicholas grew up.

"Tell me Baldwin and I promise I shall listen quietly."

"Disperkel..."

"What does that mean?"

"That's listening to me, is it?" asked Baldwin.

"Sorry Father," said Nicholas.

"Disperkel is the name of the guardian, because that is what he does. He gets rid of people by making anyone with any evil in their thoughts ill and unable to continue across the bridge. They think they are dying or going to fall over the edge of the bridge or become so ill that they must return to their beds. Many have been so driven by fear that they have gone straight to the hermitage and confessed all their sins. This has been quite profitable although we cannot hide the income from the Prior as many of these saints and holy men are too holy for our own good. You know quite well about the torture houses and the snake occupied cells at the castles and how many of our friends and neighbours ended their lives in such places. And how so many of their servants starved. Those Benedictine monks were and are liars, thieves and have been complicit in all of the murders, tortures and unsustainable taxes. They have been well rewarded for their sordid acts and are now feared, reviled and avoided by all who should be looking to them for help and advice. I am not a Christian as you well know Nicholas but I do know that we are all part of a higher intelligence. That is the reason I also know that these monks will suffer a worse fate than those they have made to suffer in return for material gain. Disperkel has kept us safe and will continue so to do as long as we meet his needs. Don't worry, there is no sacrifice, human or animal and nothing unnatural must be done for him or to him. I saw your expression change, but do you think that Tristen would conjure a spirit that required any such thing? A Pridias and Melusine Lady would do nothing so dreadful. I have told you before that when we pass, we literally pass to our own lands with our own ancestors and Disperkel lives in both worlds and he is only visible properly when there is no night or day. Tonight, is such a night."

They renewed their drinks and Baldwin continued.

"When we built the bridge, it was in a particular style and only part of it is visible to the uninitiated. The only initiated are of our blood and currently there are only two of us on this side. You and me. It seems it is far more difficult to persuade a Pridias to leave the Promised Land to come here than to return there." Baldwin stabbed his finger on the table to illustrate his point.

Baldwin got up and threw his fur cloak about his shoulders then tossed Nicholas his. They both looked tall and superior in their black and gold tunics and carrying heavy, gleaming crystal-hilted swords. Their high-ranking soldiers wore a black and gold chevron over-vest to identify them from the Cardinhams or the Turstins or any of the other Cornish families of old. Baldwin had ensured that all his men, women and horses kept themselves tidy and polished even during the darkest of the Stephonian times.

The two men went outside into the snow and Nicholas began to head over to the stables but Baldwin put a hand on his arm and held him back.

"We shall walk Nicholas, it's too cold to leave the horses by the bridge and the walk will do us both good."

Nicholas was conscious of his limp and thought that his father might have been a little more considerate instead of forcing him to walk. The damage to his leg had occurred during his traumatic birth and Nicholas was constantly aware of it, particularly when he talked to any women.

But, he was respectful of his father and so strode eastwards with him across the cliff top fields towards Ponts Mill. They descended through the woods to the path at the cliff top where the hermitage sat. It was built into the rocks, the cliff face forming the back and sides and roof of the chapel. The front was stone built with a heavy oak door. In the porchway hung a lamp which held a large candle. The small stained glass windows reflected the candles which burnt inside. The hermitage had been built in the style of their own chapel at Pridias Hall, only smaller.

The hermitage was protected by a castellated wall, one side of which extended to the bridge. The bridge was stone built with oak gates at either end and patrolled by a guard who used the stone gate house as a base. The bridge walls were castellated and tall and the tiny cottages along either side of the bridge floor were occupied by loyal Pridias tenants. Because it was the highest crossing place of the River Par before it fell into the sea, it was considered a prize and had been coveted by others for the 15 years since it had been built. No one had won it from the

Pridias although it had not been for want of trying. The older bridge and earlier crossing place was near Luxulyan and was quite a round trip for anyone wanting to get to Tywardreath or Fowey who couldn't use the ferry and daren't use the causeway.

Tonight, the bridge looked at its best. The lamps at either end of the bridge and the lights in the cottage windows shone through the snowflakes and cast yellow light on the river. Just below them on the high tide, several fishing boats and two merchant ships swayed and clanked at their moorings. There were only a few people about and they wore cloaks over their heads as they trudged through the snow homewards. Baldwin and Nicholas were recognised and acknowledged as Lords of the manor by all. The ships' crew were aboard their vessels ready for the night.

Baldwin clapped his son on the back as they arrived at the bridge gate.

"My Lords!" said the guard.

"All well tonight? "asked Baldwin.

"Yes, my Lord, it is a quiet night."

"I am glad to hear it. Family well?"

"Yes, my Lord. The children are celebrating the solstice at home with the wife but some of the neighbours have gone to the moor." The guard felt safe talking to his Lord in this way. Others would have reported him to the Priory and he would have been dragged from his home and his family killed.

"I hope they have a pleasant night and I want you to know that we appreciate your working on such a night." He handed him a coin and the guard put it in his pocket quickly.

"Thank you my Lord and you also Lord Nicholas. Are you crossing the bridge tonight?"

"We would like a walk to the far end and back if that is alright with you? I like to see the cottages in the snow."

"Of course, my Lords," and he opened the gate for them.

The men entered the bridge and strolled through. Faces came to the windows or the porches and then the occupants smiled and waved when they recognised their Lordships. The tiny cottages looked so warm and cosy with smoke coming from the chimneys and lamps at the window.

"Seren and Ddu would have loved this walk," said Nicholas of their wolves.

"Not when we meet the Disperkel," said Baldwin.

They walked to the far end and just before the gate, turned to the wall to look upriver. Baldwin pointed to the sky and Nicholas saw that the eclipse had begun.

"Quick," he said to his son and opened a door in the far bridge tower which had not been visible before. He dragged Nicholas through and soon they were underneath the bridge on a previously unnoticed stone ledge. Nicholas shivered and was about to speak out, but Baldwin put his fingers to his lips.

The ledge was lit by lamps, though tended by whom, was not obvious. Suddenly a low growling noise echoed down the walls. Nicholas began to experience the freezing shivers he usually did when he thought that there was a spirit about. He envisioned that some kind of demon with his eye hanging out would soon crawl towards them, one arm outstretched and finger pointing. He must have made some sort of involuntary squealing noise because Baldwin whispered harshly,

"What is the matter with you?"

Nicholas didn't answer.

They shuffled along the ledge, holding tightly to the wall and Nicholas was conscious of his lameness and hoped they would not need a speedy getaway. They had walked so far that he imagined that they must have reached the other side of the bridge. His guess was correct as Baldwin climbed a few steps and opened a door and soon they were standing at the home gate. The guard grinned and let them out onto the path and he bid them goodnight.

"What was that for?" asked Nicholas. "We just shuffled along a narrow ledge on the outside of the bridge and we could have walked across the top?"

His father was laughing so much that he bent over.

"It's good to know about every angle of your properties!" he said.

"I thought I was to meet some horrible monster that was going to come up from the river!"

"No, he doesn't live in the river. He lives in there." And Baldwin pointed to the chapel.

Baldwin walked over to the door and knocked. It was opened immediately and they were welcomed in by a man wearing a monk's robe of grey wool brought together around his slim middle with knotted cord. He also wore a hooded grey cloak which had snow all over it.

"Been out Patrick?"

"Yes, I have, just got back in. I knew you would be here soon. Come on in quickly, the moon has almost gone."

He pulled them inside and drew the wooden bar across. Baldwin had designed the chapel this way, for with the rock face making three sides and a small securely barred door, it would be very difficult to impregnate with force. The roof overhang and the tiny glass windows completed the secure cell.

"No time to offer you a drink both. He will be here soon."

The candles went out with a strange breeze and they were in darkness. Nicholas went to the window and could no longer see the moon. In fact, he couldn't see the bridge and the houses upon it. That did not make sense as there was no reason not to see the cottage lamps. Before he could successfully work through the problem he was aware of a change in the atmosphere of the room. His skin was crawling and he was so cold.

"Nicholas, will you turn around?" asked Baldwin.

As he did, Nicholas saw his father standing next to the hooded monk. Baldwin was laughing and pointing at the monk's face. Nicholas moved closer and closer until he was directly in front of the man.

"Go on! Move his hood back!"

"No, I daren't!"

Baldwin put his hand to the cloak hood and gently lifted it backwards. There was nothing there, no one. Nicholas froze. A little light came in through the window as the moon began to escape its own cloak. As it did so, a skull began to appear in the hood space where there had been nothing before. The moon gradually became brighter and as it did, flesh appeared upon the skull bit by bit. By the time the moon was again free of its shadow, the monk was returned to life.

"What have I just witnessed?" Nicholas asked breathlessly.

"I am the Disperkel," said the monk. "I protect you lot!"

Baldwin was still laughing, he enjoyed the trick.

"My son, I know I told you of a terrible demon, but although our friend is a strange man I agree, he is quite safe to us."

The monk removed his cloak and folded it neatly onto the table. He held out his hands to Baldwin who took them gladly and shook them.

"This monk will live here forever, so long as there are people of our blood in this land. If they leave he will wait until a Pridias returns to the land again. He has prevented the followers of the Devil King from reaching us."

"Forever. You will protect us forever?" asked Nicholas.

"I will and I will be here even after the sea retreats expanding the land to the edge of the bay."

"He always says that," confided Baldwin.

"The sea will move away from here and the land will rise. Your Pridias Hall will one day sit a long way back from the cliffs, leaving fields and roads and many houses and people. It will retreat far back from the Priory and there will be no harbours or ships up here. I might not like it here quite so much then but Tristen has said that I must stay."

"Oh. Right," said Nicholas.

"Come on home boy. You have met our Disperkel now and can visit anytime you like."

"And ask you questions about God?"

"Not God boy. Not as the Priory monks tell you. The chapel monks' faces will change over the years, but the Disperkel will always be behind his mask. God doesn't come into it."

The men walked back out into the snow and the jolly hermit monk closed the door again.

"So, he is an actual spirit guard?"

"He is. Isn't he great?"

"I suppose so. He wasn't really who I imagined I was going to meet."

"That is because your soul is pretty good. If it wasn't, your experience would be of hell itself."

Baldwin and Nicholas walked home by the coast path. The tide was moving out and the beach and rock pools just becoming visible in the bright moonlight. The snow still fell, but their fur cloaks kept them warm. Ships at sea were visible as a shadow silhouette and cottage lamps burned brightly against the dark walls. Looking across the bay they could see twinkling cottage lights there too. The brightest lights came from the Priory and the pier front at Tywardreath.

"The Priory is wasting our money on lamps and candles again," muttered Nicholas.

"It seems odd when the Disperkel tells us about all of this being land," said Baldwin, waving his arm in the general direction of the sea.

"He must be a witch of some sort to know that," mused Nicholas

"He's a good man. A good Disperkel."

They laughed and turned uphill to walk back to the Hall. It wasn't until they were enjoying a meal later that night when Nicholas realised that he was no longer lame.

THE HANGED MAN

Featuring Nicholas de Pridias

(1135 – 1200)

Nicholas was regretting yet again having been persuaded by Alana to do it, but every time he mentioned it to her, she would flounce out of the hall and say that she could never understand him. How the moaning woman could say that was beyond him. She was more than aware of the things he had done to keep her and their lands safe.

He married Alana Cardinham in 1158 as the final solution to the skirmishes between their families in hope that peace could break out. Osbert, the Prior at Tywardreath had intervened and with a substantial financial payment from Cardinham's father and from Baldwin de Pridias worked out a contract that even the new King could not fault.

Sadly, the couple did not get on and once Alana had produced the twin boys Richard and Herden, their roles had been fulfilled and they lived separate lives. Alana spent a great deal of time at Restormel and it was at Nicholas's insistence that the boys remained at Pridias with their wet nurses.

The King Henry, who was a small improvement on the last, nevertheless had troubles of his own and had several times called upon his Lords to assist him in France while he fought to restore lands there. Nicholas has been forced at 47 years of age, to travel with twenty Pridias fighters to fight for their King. Nicholas had received the princely sum of half a mark for his expenses which were many times more than that. The journey across the sea with the horses on the boats was troubling enough but luckily, they all arrived safely and no man nor horse were lost in the battle.

Nicholas was glad to return to Pridias where he regaled his family and friends with stories, not too embellished, about their travels and was ignorant of the fire he had lit in the minds of his sons. This was around the time that Alana went from Ladylike indifference to open hostility towards her husband. She had enjoyed free reign while he was in France.

The boys had been competing locally in tournaments and now wanted to train in order that they could compete around the country. Nicholas then told them of the young King Henry who was to be trained by the renowned William Marshal and they were mesmerised.

If truth be told, Nicholas had also become more than interested in the fun and had assigned a tutor to his young sons from among his own ranks of men. They would practice for hours along the cliff top meadows, from Pridias to Biscovey.

By 1189, the boys, now men, were both married. They often travelled to France and remained there for months at a time, following the tournaments wherever they led. Richard was the father of a nine-year-old boy, but the weaker Herden had no children. Neither minded leaving their families or their lands, the first Pridias generation to do so for a considerable time.

Henry Fitz Count the Earl, had demanded that at the young Richard must remain in Cornwall and be ready to fight or work for the King and take his duties as a Lord seriously. Richard was the first-born twin and so Herden was deemed freer to leave.

"There are already four Pridias Lords available for him!" complained Richard. "You, me, Herden and my boy Richard. If Herden ever gets his own wife with child, then there will be more! I want to be in France where I am making a fortune collecting ransoms. More than we make on this rotten bit of land. Make Herden stay!"

Nicholas had put his foot down and Richard responded by leaving his son with Nicholas and taking his wife Guinevere, his horses and his men to France. Nicholas then had the bright idea of passing off Herden as Richard to avoid fines and this worked for a long time. They were finally discovered when news began to arrive at Cornwall that Richard de Pridias was doing so well in France and Spain.

Twice Nicholas had been fined for making false claims about his sons, but the Earl was sympathetic, having boys of his own. Following the second fine of 1192, Nicholas sent a stiff message to Richard, who did not receive it as he was already on his way home, having badly injured his leg at the Tournament. When he returned and was lying at Pridias Hall with his wilful wife looking after him and their connection renewed with their now twelve-year-old son, Nicholas told him that if he did not stay at Pridias he would be disinherited.

Herden, who had been manfully and willingly looking after their estates while his ridiculous brother had been away on his jollies, took himself into the woods and hung himself from an oak tree. Alana blamed Nicholas and blamed Richard and blamed Guinevere, the slut of a wife she considered her to be.

Today, Alana had come into Nicholas's study to inform him that she had seen Herden in the woods and he had spoken to her. Nicholas did not believe her, which he realised was a little mean as he knew full well that such things could and did happen. Now that she had left him alone, he felt guilty and wished he had his father to confide in. He would have known what to do, although times had changed everything so much that he felt that once he died, memories and links to the old days would be gone. His own children had been such disappointments.

It wasn't as though he didn't have enough to worry about. Even the lands were now referred to the Manor of Pridias of Priory of Tywardreath and his son Richard did not seem to care or understand. The new King Richard spent a lot of time abroad or planning to go abroad and needed a goodly amount of income. William de Wrotham had been given the task of raising money from tin mining in Devon and Cornwall by Hubert Walter, the Archbishop of Canterbury. He was appointed the First Lord Warden of the Stannaries on 20th November 1197.

These new laws meant that anyone connected with tin mining could only deal with the stannary courts and were exempt from Parliament in London. In some ways, it was helpful and in others meant that Nicholas's mining interests were being badly affected by local political influence.

Nicholas was looking through some of his current holdings and was wondering how he could add to them,

Great and Little Pridias,
Lestoon,
Levrean,
Rosemullen,
Trevanney,
Trenince,
Ponts Mill in Luxulyan.
Stenalees in St Austell,
Grediow in Lanlivery,
Biscovay in Landreath,
Carroget,
Kilhalland,
Rosegarth,
Penpillick in Tywardreath.
Gubbavean in St Issey,
Nanscowe in St Breaock,
moieties in Golant,
Bakers.

It was becoming more difficult so to do, with the Prior and the monks controlling so much of what went on in the area and the secret political alignments that were tricky to foretell.

He got up from his desk and walked over to the window. He could see his Lordly line altogether in the walled garden, an addition he had decided to create after seeing so many wonderful gardens in the south of France when he had been there. It was ironic that his son Richard now found such pleasure in furthering its creation rather than gallivanting abroad.

There, playing some kind of ball game were his 40-year-old son and his wife Guinevere, their son Richard, now 20 with his wife Morgana who held their new born son Geoffrey. Richard and Morgana had married at 16 and were already the parents of two boys, Baldwin and Reginald who were playing around the garden too. They were laughing and relaxed and enjoying themselves. That was until he saw Alana stride into the garden, still nimble in spite of her 60 years and apparently announce to them that Herden was haunting the woods.

He would have to go out and join them.

Nicholas was not as nimble as his wife, his worries and the fighting in France had affected his stamina. His healer told him that his heart was sad and wanted to go home. Nicholas could not argue with that and as there were four generations of Pridias Lords alive, he knew that he could leave the estates in... That was his problem, he did not consider Richard to be a pair of safe hands.

Baldwin would have known what to do and the only way he knew to ask him was to die and then it would be too late.

By the time Nicholas reached the garden, the party had split.

"The Richards have gone for horses so that they can check the woods for Herden," said Alana, arms folded and triumph in her voice.

"I shall join them," said Nicholas and turned to go.

"I shouldn't bother my beloved husband, you cared nothing for him when he was alive and rewarded his devotion and hard work with rejection."

"Herden was weak and he sulked rather too much for a Pridias. If he hadn't been a twin of Richard, I might have doubted his origins."

Alana walked towards her husband as though she would strike him and then thought better of it. Nicholas may well strike her back.

"He was your son Nicholas. As much of a son as Richard is."

"Herden was the one who kept reporting us to the Priory, you know that don't you? He would have had me imprisoned if he had not been stopped."

"I don't believe you."

"It's true. He killed himself because he knew I had found out, nothing else."

Alana walked to Morgana who was clutching Geoffrey, frightened of the scene she was witnessing. She handed the child to his grandmother when she held out her hands.

"Sweet, sweet baby boy," said Alana and Morgana stood, nervously awaiting the safe return of her son.

Nicholas rode into the woods following the trackway he guessed his boys had taken. He was accompanied by Alain and William, two of his men who he hoped would help him with this unusual search. He had not needed to explain, for gossip had shot through the Hall and its surrounds when Alana came home crying and screaming.

A few minutes into the woods, they came across the two Richards, the youngest of whom put a finger to his lips as they arrived. He pointed in front of them and they could see what he could see, a man hanging by the neck from the same oak tree that Herden had killed himself. This man was decomposing and stinking and swinging.

Nicholas put his hand to his mouth to suppress a shout. His son and grandson were frozen on their horses that stood stock still. His men dismounted and walked bravely and deliberately to the swinging corpse. They could not recognise the body because the head was weathered and the tongue black and extended. The man was naked and could not be identified by his clothes.

"Shall we cut him down sir?" asked William.

"Yes, yes indeed. Who is it?" said Nicholas.

"It is Herden," said his son. "He was speaking when we arrived."

"What nonsense!" exclaimed Nicholas.

"I am telling you Father. That swinging corpse spoke to us and said that he was Herden."

"He knew our names," added Richard junior.

"Everyone around here knows our names," pointed out Nicholas, eager to remain the sensible leader.

"But he's a corpse. I think that makes a difference," said his son.

The servants laid out the said corpse and manfully refrained from gagging at the stench.

"You two must have been overexcited after Alana said she had seen Herden. I do not recognise this corpse so ask around and find out if anyone knows him. Then take his body to Tywardreath and have the monks deal with it. I will not be accused of covering up any deaths."

Alain remained with the body and William returned with the others so that he could collect a cart. Nicholas searched for his wife on their return to the Hall to tell her that she was mistaken. He could not find her and was informed that no one knew of her current whereabouts. While he searched for her in the tower which faced the sea, a favourite haunt of hers, he noticed how rough the sea was becoming. Even though their bay was relatively sheltered, the little ships were still struggling to stay on course. He saw on the west bank at Biscovey that a bonfire was lit and he wondered vaguely why. It was away from the houses there, but very large. The wind and rain which looked like it was on its way would soon put it out, he thought.

There was a hammering on the door and Nicholas opened it.

"Sorry my Lord, the Lords Richard have asked that you come down to the courtyard. Something funny has happened they said."

Nicholas followed the servant down the steps and outside where he found his son, grandson and Alain and William. The cart containing the body was in the middle of the yard and not on its way across Baldwin's Bridge and down to Tywardreath.

"What's going on?" he asked.

"It spoke again, my Lord. It said it was Herden and had come to say he was sorry."

"Really it did, my Lord," added William.

It seemed they had put the body on the cart, covered it with sacking and set off for the bridge. They followed the river down from the woods on the rutted track and were horrified when the sacking began moving and a voice came from it. They jumped off the cart and drew their swords and used one of them to raise the brown sacking. The voice continued repeating, 'Sorry, I am so very sorry.' They were sure it came from the corpse but when they looked at his leathery face there was no sign of life or speech.

"Just like we heard, what do you think it means?"

Nicholas stopped for a moment and then asked, "Why do you think it was Herden?"

"The voice was his, my Lord!" Nods all round meant they all believed that to be so.

"I am sorry!" was the wail from under the sacking and to a man they jumped backwards.

"Pull that cover off!" instructed Nicholas.

His son gingerly pulled it off and revealed the decaying corpse with a voice emitting from the blackened mouth. It was saying over and over again.

"I am sorry, I shouldn't have told them and I shouldn't have killed myself. I didn't mean to hurt Mother."

Alana was listening now and crying,

"Herden! My boy!"

Richard said, "This isn't right!"

"I am not dead, I cannot leave without forgiveness!"

"Nothing to forgive, little Hickadon!" said Alana, resorting to her baby name for the boy.

He stopped talking and Nicholas beckoned that the sack be put over him again.

"We must perform another service at the chapel!" said Alana. "Fetch the monks, they will have to be involved."

"We have already buried him once, they won't do it again! They can't!"

"Should we check that he is in the chapel before we make fools of ourselves?" asked Richard junior, quite reasonably.

"Good thinking," said his father and led the way to the chapel that had witnessed weddings, christenings, burials and spells. The normally closed door was open, the chapel waiting for them and they entered.

"The candles have gone out," noted Nicholas. "Light them, William."

As soon as light was thrown around the dimly lit room, the storm began outside. The rain was sideways and torrential and the temperature had dropped sharply. Cloaks were being pulled tighter around shoulders and held there with folded arms. No one was feeling secure.

Nicholas took his Lordly role again and went down to the crypt. The family had the chapel extended underground and lined with stone in order to keep the Pridias bodies intact. Jehanne and Tristen had taken care of bodies in a different way to Alana and the other women who knew nothing about the old ways. Now death meant an oak coffin sealed into a stone sarcophagus for preservation.

Nicholas reached for a step and climbed it so that he could touch Herden's coffin.

"Let me, Father. Please," said his son. "Go back upstairs and Richard and I will deal with this."

Nicholas glad of the excuse to be relieved of this gruesome task, left the men alone.

"What are we going to find?" asked Richard the younger.

"Not a clue," said his father and took the metal bar from its shelf and began to dislodge the mortar from around the lid. His son joined him using a pickaxe. In testament to the workmen who had constructed the sarcophagus, it took a long time to remove the lid. Laying bare the oak coffin released such a smell that they could not deny that a decomposing body lay inside.

They held their noses and tried to stop gagging.

"Shall I?" asked the younger.

"No, but catch me if I fall," said his father.

He prised the oak top and it broke free, breaking rather than coming off in one piece. It soon revealed the corpse of a man that was once his twin brother. He was wearing his black and gold tunic and his fur cloak. It was Herden.

"Who is on the cart then?"

"I have no clue," said his father. "Fetch Lord Nicholas."

Nicholas arrived with Alana hanging on to his arm, eyes wide with anticipation.

"Is your brother there, Richard?"

"Yes, Mother. Herden is in his tomb."

"I want to see," she said. Before they could stop her, she was on the step and peering into the coffin. She stepped off quietly and made her stately way upstairs to the chapel.

"Shall I close it now?" asked the younger.

"I suppose so. Whoever is in the cart, it's not my twin brother."

The younger Richard began repositioning the lid and pulling the stones back.

"I'll get the mason to fix it tomorrow."

They went upstairs and found the rest of the family.

"We are going to tell Alain and William to take it to the Priory tomorrow. Let them deal with it," Nicholas informed them.

"We thought we would let the masons finish clearing up in the crypt," said Richard.

"We should do another service for Herden," insisted Alana. "Help him rest."

Morgana nodded and the women huddled together collecting candles and incense,

"We need a monk," said Alana.

"We can manage without, Alana," said her daughter-in-law. Alana nodded, weakened by recent events.

Nicholas and the Richards followed their men outside, hoods up, the weather still raw and determined. They strode over to the cart.

"Better get it under cover," instructed Nicholas. "Perhaps the body could melt or dissolve in this weather."

Richard the elder lifted the sacking and dropped it again. He turned to look at the others and then turned back to the cart. He lifted the sacking and stared. There lay a dead pig. A pig that had been dead for a long time.

"It's a pig," said Nicholas.

"I don't understand," said the younger.

"We can't take it to the Priory," said the elder.

"No."

"We should burn it or the wolves will dig it up and I don't want them poisoned by this weird pig-man-devil thing," Nicholas insisted.

"There's a fire at Biscovey, lets tip it there tonight. I don't want it here any longer than I need to."

"Is the fire still going? In this rain?"

"It was a pretty big fire."

William jumped on the cart seat, "I will take it, my Lord."

"We will come with you."

That was the procession which moved quickly from Pridias, down the cliff path and south to Biscovey to the edge of the bay. Three Lords, two men servants and a cart carrying a decomposing pig, cantering through the torrential rain. As they arrived at the site of the fire, they found two men tending the blaze.

"We are burning the old bedding from the barns, my Lords. It was dry when we started but this storm blew up and we daren't stop tending it."

"We have something which will help it burn," said Alain and he and William took both ends of the sacking and threw the bundle on to the fire. Within a few minutes the spitting began and the group stood back a little to watch. As the fire glowed brighter and spat there was a general feeling that a problem had been solved. Asking no questions of their Lordships, the workmen promised to remain with the fire until all evidence was gone and so the Pridias group trotted homewards.

When they reached Landreath, they heard an explosion behind. They all turned and saw a huge pall of smoke and ball of flame shoot into the sky. The giant spirit image of Herden appeared in the air. Its mouth opened and screamed and then it vanished, leaving only a large bonfire.

"Don't tell the women," instructed Lord Nicholas.

The men rode home.

Lord Nicholas of the tired heart died in his bed the following day.

THE JOUSTING LORDS

Featuring Richard de Pridias

(1160 -1225)

Travelling around France with his horses and men was the best fun Richard had ever had. Guinevere coming along was interesting too. He would rather that had she remained at Pridias with the baby, but she had insisted that she accompany him, citing his wellbeing. Everyone knew that it was because she didn't want him enjoying himself with the women, beautiful young women, who liked to follow the knights and their entourage around the tournament circuit. That was a shame, as he was partial to young women. Guinevere was good company however and supported him in whatever he did.

Richard first got interested in the sport after his Royal sojourn with his father and the King. Until then, he hadn't realised that he could be so good at anything. He loved the sound of the cheers and the claps of the crowd. Richard had always been a good rider, excelling at the kind of paces that worked well with music. He often made one of the servants play while he rode at Pridias so that he could improve his timing. He was a great swordsman and archer and so he had only to master jousting. He had practised and practiced with his tutor and Herden and improved every time.

Herden was a different matter. He was quite a good rider, but weak at the sword and bow. He practised with Richard, taking on all the instruction and advice and ended up a poor second. When their soldiers joined in, Herden would move down the rankings - he was always last. They had never used a sparring partner who finished lower than Herden. But Herden seemed unaffected by his poor skills and was just happy to compete.

Therein lay the problem. They both went to France on the first tournament circuit and enjoyed it as much as each other. On their return home, they talked of their successes and fame and popularity and the money they had earned. They were equally proud of their achievements, although Richard had evidently earned the most. They returned for the seventh season and Herden was getting better and had been placed in several competitions. He had beaten Richard on a couple of occasions and Richard was beating some good knights. He really felt that he was beginning to make his mark. One more season should do it.

The instruction was then sent down from the Earl that Richard must remain in England and Herden would be allowed to go to France, Herden was excited. Handsome Herden would now be lauded instead of handsome Richard. Richard pouted, sulked, complained and finally left with his wife, horses and men on an early tide, giving Herden little choice in the matter.

Then the supposedly impartial Nicholas came up with the scheme of passing off Herden as Richard in order to avoid punishments and the ruination of their own good name. Herden eventually agreed, and only the closest personal servants were aware of the switch. Herden began to enjoy the role, not realising until this point that his brother was treated far better locally than he ever had been. It might be good to be Richard for a while.

Herden had two separate blow ups with his father, once when he was not allowed to make decisions on some horse purchases from a Spanish merchant and second when his father discovered that Herden had been using one of the young daughters of a woodsman in a most ungentlemanly way. She had been too frightened to tell and it was her mother who discovered the outrage and walked directly to Lord Nicholas and told him to do something about it. He published Herden financially, not wishing to report him to the Priory and paid the woodsman's family off. Both times, Herden complained to the Priory that Richard had gone to France and twice Nicholas was fined. The Earl of Cornwall was more irritated by Herden and his obnoxious ways than the transgressions of Nicholas, but had to be seen to punish Nicholas in some way. None of it helped the family dynamics.

Richard, currently in Rouen, had no knowledge of these domestic upsets and was getting ready to meet his next opponent, who if he beat would earn him enough money to finish the season. It was a funny thing recently, although he was having so much fun, home was calling. His son Richard, the sea, the woods - even his father.

Guinevere came skipping into the stable.

"Is Perseus ready? Oh, he is! Let me straighten everything, he looks so lovely!" Guinevere fussed over the grey stallion, beloved of everyone in the Pridias team. She straightened his coverings, polished his leather and kissed him on the nose. They had four horses with them now, all capable of winning, so long as their master could do his job properly. They were worth a good deal of money and Richard had been offered a King's ransom for Perseus, the best of them all. Richard intended breeding from him as soon as they were all home and that was one of the plans on his mind. Horses were hurt in this sport, some badly and he didn't want that fate for Perseus, or any of them for that matter.

"Don't baby him Gwen," he said.

"Baby him? I look after him so that he looks after you, my lovely husband," she laughed.

They kissed and Perseus pushed them with his nose. His squire ran in and said breathlessly,

"Lord Marshal has asked if there can be a delay, my Lord."

"No! If he is not ready, then he must take the forfeit!"

"His horse has been stolen, my Lord."

"That is the third one this week," said Guinevere.

"Yes, it is becoming a worry," admitted Richard. "Tell me John, does anyone have any idea of how this calamity happened?"

"It seems not, my Lord, but as sure as anything the thieves will take one too many and then they will pay for it."

"You must maintain a guard on all of the horses and particularly this one here," said Richard pointing to the grey.

"I would never let anything happen to the horses. I would die first, my Lord."

"I will guard them too," added Guinevere defiantly.

Richard smiled at his team, this was real brotherhood he thought. Working together, not in competition as he had been with his own brother.

"Tell Lord Marshal, I shall wait until he is ready. I presume he has other horses?"

"I do Lord Pridias. I have two other horses, but it will take a while to get one ready, perhaps 30 minutes. The organisers have given their permission so long as you agree. If you do not, you may take the win as my forfeit." Marshal had entered the stables with his squire and two men.

"It is no honour to me to take your forfeit, Lord Marshal."

"I might have taken it the other way about," he answered.

"I doubt it. I shall be out soon and then I shall beat you on the field."

Richard did beat Marshal. His second horse was neither so fast nor agile and was probably tired from his outings that morning. Richard felt the thrill as he always did when he galloped with his lance towards his opponent. At the first strike, he knew that Marshal was not as strong as he usually was and although the pass went to Richard, he did not go so hard on the second pass. It felt like he was taking advantage somehow. So, he won, but felt the cheers and the applause not quite as deserved as they might be.

As he rode back to the stables, Perseus still prancing under his body, he saw a face he recognised in the crowd. He couldn't remember where he had seen this man, but felt that he was not a good man.

"There is a man over there John. The one with the red beard and odd looking boots, standing by the pie seller. Can you see him?"

"Yes, my Lord."

"Do you recognise him?"

"I am sure he was at the last tour... in fact I am sure he is friends with Cholmondeley's squire. Shall I speak to him before you do?"

"No, no John, But I would be very interested in finding out what he has been up to lately."

"You think he is something to do with the thefts?"

"I do John and I couldn't tell you why I think it."

They got back to the stables and Guinevere was there, talking closely to one of their servants, James. They moved apart as Richard rode in and Guinevere said,

"James has something to tell you Richard."

"Oh yes?" said her husband, using the block to dismount.

"My Lord, I have been given some information about the people who are stealing horses."

"Not so much been given the information Richard, as he beat it out of him."

Handsome and blushing James bowed his head and then looked at his master. Richard saw that James was in love with his wife, but worried not. Guinevere would not be unfaithful to him, he could guarantee that.

"Tell me, James."

James told Richard of his visit to one of the taverns in town where he had been informed by a Frenchman that bets were being taken against the expected outcome of challenges. It seemed that some men were able to clean up with bets against the favourites and this phenomenon was being linked to the recent spate of sword and saddle thefts or similar. Now the horse thefts had added to the odds against a champion. Bets on the reliable constant winners were not resulting in a profit, they no longer had the edge.

"Do you know who is behind it?"

"Joachim of Aquitaine."

"Really?" Richard was surprised to hear this. Joachim was a well-known competitor, but not that successful.

"They say he began by sending his squires to steal so that he could sell and bring in some cash. His father will not release any more money to him and the servants needed to steal in order to eat. Then Aquitaine got bigger ideas and has now been selling the horses for breeding. It seems not everyone is worried about using stolen animals to improve their tournament stock. Then he soon realised that he could earn more money through betting scams. He's stupid though because he's crossing people who will kill him."

"I will kill him if he takes anything of ours," said Guinevere.

"He won't," said Richard and he instructed John to take care of the horses and he beckoned his wife to accompany him.

He walked with her directly to Joachim's tent and walked in. A servant followed them inside and asked what they were doing.

"Looking for my friend. Where is he?"

"My Lord, he is not here at the moment. Shall I tell him you called?"

"I will find him later," said Richard.

They were soon joined in the tent by the man Richard had noticed after his event. The man seemed surprised to see Richard there but soon recovered his composure and said,

"You did well today, my Lord."

"Thank you, thank you."

"Your horse is a wonderful beast, are you intending to use him for breeding? I would be interested in using him."

Richard squeezed Guinevere's hand to keep her quiet.

"No, no. I don't think so."

"I understand, my Lord, and red beard bowed.

They left and Richard had a feeling he would be dealing with the man again. He certainly felt that he was being watched.

"We all stay with our stuff from now on. At least until we have the thieves sorted."

Two nights later, they had their chance. Joachim Aquitaine and the man with the beard and the odd boots, who they discovered was called Philippe la Garre, called late one evening and seemed surprised to find everyone at the stables. Not only were the Pridias team, but the Marshals and the Cholmondeleys, all of whom had suffered recent thefts, were working a shift pattern of guard duties. In fact, they were currently having a meeting about how to proceed and were amazed that Aquitaine had shown his hand so swiftly.

"Gentleman! Ah, I see my Lady Guinevere is also here!"

"Why are you here?" asked Marshal.

"I came only for a walk on a lovely night," he answered.

They had just been discussing how Joachim had apparently recently received news that there would be no money and that he was to be disinherited because of his debts. Once Marshal had discovered who had likely taken his horse, he was apoplectic. All the competitors loved their horses – really loved their horses.

"Do you know anything of the missing horses, Joachim?" Marshal asked him.

"Of course not, William. How should I? You must be most upset that your lovely bay has gone. He was such a good ride."

"How would you know? No one has ridden him other than me or my squire?"

Joachim shifted his feet and the atmosphere in the room became tense. La Garre put his hand on his dagger in its sheath and the tension exploded. Marshal leapt across the stall and held his sword across Joachim's throat.

"Where is he?"

"Who?" he asked.

Before there were any more words, La Garre drew his own dagger and went for Marshal. Richard grabbed him around the neck and so La Garre turned on him. Within a few seconds the man was dead and Richard held the bloody dagger. Joachim Aquitaine began to cry out and Marshal stabbed him.

"Where is my horse, you bastard?"

"I do not know and if I did, I would not tell an English pig such as you."

Marshal slit Aquitaine's throat and the stunned vigilante group looked at the bodies. Squire John ripped sacking from the stall sides and threw it over the dead men. The action spurred the others on and soon the bodies were wrapped, tied and hidden on a cart. One of Marshal's men brought in a pig's carcass and threw it on top of the bodies.

"Now search his place and stables before anyone realises he is missing," instructed Richard.

"I will go too," said Guinevere.

Guinevere moved majestically between the tents and the men and the horses, accompanied by the squire John and William Marshal and two of his men. They couple chattered innocently between themselves as they made their way directly to Aquitaine's camp. When they arrived, there were only two boys looking after the horses.

"Is your master here?" asked Marshal.

"No, my Lord. He went to fetch another horse he has bought and then he is coming back."

"He must have great faith in you to leave you with his horses?"

"Yes, my Lady. He does."

"Have you been with him long?"

"Only a week, my Lady. His last servants went to work for another Knight."

"Well, we shall return later when your master is back. I am buying some horses from him and he was to let us ride them today," said Marshal. "It's a pity he is not here, as we may not all been able to see them until tomorrow."

"Perhaps you could let us look now? It would save us all time and I know my Lord Aquitaine is keen to sell the horses and we have money to buy them," asked Guinevere. Marshal rattled his money pouch for effect.

"We could give you some coins for your time and trouble?" said Guinevere brightly.

The servant children grinned and held out their hands. Satisfied, they led the group to the stables. Of the three horses there, Marshal went to the quiet animal at the back which was covered by a dull rug. The horse recognised him immediately and Marshal had to stop the tears which came to his eyes.

"We are going home now," he whispered in its ear and he quickly removed the rug. He flinched when he saw the whip marks on his flanks.

"My Lord?" said his own man. "These other horses belong to Cholmondeley and Mortimer. They have their markings."

"Saddle them, take them back to their owners," he instructed.

"Are you taking the horses now, my Lord?" asked the Aquitaine servant boys.

"Yes, tell your master we have taken them when he returns." He threw the boys extra coins and they vanished.

Once the horses were back with their owners and the bodies burned, Richard decided that he had had enough. His leg was really hurting him after the fight and the deaths had shaken him. He didn't feel guilty about the deaths, just that Guinevere had been involved. She seemed to have enjoyed herself however and was really pleased to have been part of retrieving the horses. Their fellow jousters and competitors and friends said nothing about the disappearance of Joachim Aquitaine and his lackeys, telling any enquirers that they knew he had been short of money and deeply in debt and had perhaps just vanished and begun a new life in Italy or somewhere. If they knew the truth, they weren't saying.

But it still seemed the right time to go home and his wife agreed. They all made their way to the coast where they rented a ship capable of carrying them and their horses and sailed home, eventually docking at Ponts Mill. Richard did not tell Guinevere or any of his men that he had seen two men following them on horses to the Brittany coast. On one of their overnight camps, he had left the group and gone in search of the men, but seen no one. He began to feel as though he were imagining it and assumed that God punished differently when He considered a death murder, rather than a battle death. Was dying in battle somehow nobler? He hadn't thought so until recently.

Richard became more alarmed when they sailed across the sea to Cornwall and he thought he saw the two men in a boat a way behind. He chose to ignore them. When they arrived at Ponts Mill, he insisted that they moor on the eastern side of the river citing his desire to cross his grandfather's bridge and cleanse the whole group at the hermitage chapel. There were no arguments and no troubles as the tired men, woman and horses disembarked on the quay. He asked one of the men at the quayside to lend them a cart upon which they could load their possessions and the driver could haul them the short distance home. When the gatekeeper opened the bridge gate and bowed low, they entered and began to cross the bridge. Tenants who were home shouted greetings to Richard and Guinevere. Richard looked behind and noticed the guard allowing unseen travellers on to the bridge behind them.

By the time they reached the far side of the bridge, Richard only passed a short conversation with the guard and shooed his group through. The cart trundled behind. He could see no one at the hermitage and hoped that he would be able to make it home safely with the Disperkel stopping any demons following.

"Where is the hermit monk?" he asked the guard.

"He was called to the Priory, my Lord. Your Father and Mother will be very pleased to see you. Are you home for good now, my Lord?"

"We are," answered Guinevere.

So, the Disperkel monk was not there to save him from these spirit horsemen, that was not good news.

They made their way up the track and through the woods to the Hall. Richard looked behind as they went through the entrance gate in the walls and thought he caught the shape of two riders in the woods. He was brought back from his musings as soon as their return was announced to the family and they were overwhelmed with welcome.

When Herden galloped off into the woods in his huff after Richard's reinstatement as Lord in waiting, it had not been expected that he would kill himself. But suicide was the accepted verdict and he was buried in the family crypt.

Richard never saw the two shadow riders again after Herden's death and he resolutely put out of his mind that Herden in his gold and black tunic looked exactly the same as Richard did in his.

THE PRIESTESS

Featuring Richard de Pridias

(1180 – 1250)

My dear Geoffrey,

I feel that I must explain my behaviour on your last visit and apologise. It was good to see you and Isabella and the boys, although they are no longer boys, are they? Roger 12 and Piers 9, time goes so quickly. We always say that as adults and yet it is such a true statement. I feel old lately and your brother tells me that I must get used to it. I still feel as though I am a young man and yet your brother has been taking over more of the responsibilities of the Manor, without informing me. Our income has gone down so much in recent years with these new mining laws and the sons of our workers would rather leave the land than farm it. I find it all so confusing and wonder how much longer I can put up with it. Baldwin tells me that the lands are safe in his hands but we both know how selfish he is. He likes spending money and has redecorated his own hall with such splendour I wonder where he imagines the money will come from. Reginald we never see, now that he is such an important lawyer. I have heard tell that the Bishop is very impressed with him. He certainly gives him some favourable cases and I am not sure that Reginald is too interested in what is the best for the Cornish. He mentions Rome and the Church far too often for my liking. I want the old ways, but we are no longer able to mention them. People have forgotten. She has told me that soon those ways will vanish from our world.

Your father

Richard
Lord of Pridias

Father,

You do not need to apologise. However, you did not explain in the letter what the trouble was. Perhaps you can let me know more in your next letter. Isabella and I really enjoy our visits home, although I must say Orcherton seems so much warmer after rainy and misty Pridias. When Pridias is at its best with the hot sun and the beach and the clear sea, there is no better place on earth. But, Devon is so green and the rocks are so warm and red and I fell in love with it the first day I arrived. I want to visit Cornwall often and am sad that our parting was so very uncomfortable. Isabella and Roger and Piers send their love. By the way - Who is she?

Geoffrey

Baldwin,

I had a strange letter from Father by messenger today and have sent a reply separate to this letter. Is he alright? You know how odd he was on my last visit with my wife and the children, insisting that they were foreigners and the like. He said he wanted to explain and then he didn't and he mentioned some woman. Perhaps I am making a fuss but I just wanted to check. He is still going on about Reg and his lawyering, I think he is worried the connection with the Church and their interference at Pridias. Are you and the family going to come over to Orcherton soon? You will love it here.

Geoffrey and Isabella.

Brother dear,

Father is getting old, that's half the trouble and don't worry about Reginald. He is learning what he can, where he can and is making waves and lots of money in the meantime. Reginald is not remotely religious and cares little about Bishops and monks, he cares only about money. That is not a bad thing, I could certainly do with more money. Father says I spend too much, when all I am trying to do is bring the place up to the present day. Father does so live in the 11th century and wants to tell me about protecting spirits and relics buried in the grounds and Melusine bloodlines. It's all nonsense of course, all that matters is today. I don't know who this she is, unless he's getting religious fever and is talking about the Virgin Mary. I am not speaking out of turn, but I think he has been around long enough and should go and join his ancestors. We will come when we have some spare time, my wife is currently awaiting another arrival.

Baldwin

Father,

I hope you got my last letter. It has been two months and I have heard nothing from you. I do worry and I cannot help it. Shall I come home for a while? Everyone is well here and send their love.

Geoffrey and Isabella.

Father,

Another month has passed and I think that I should come back to Pridias. I have written to Baldwin too and he has not replied. If you are not careful, I shall write to Reginald and then we shall all be in a pickle! Please write soon, I have asked this messenger to deliver this into your hands and insist you send me a reply.

Geoffrey

Geoffrey

The messenger delivered your letter to me, he having asked for Lord Pridias and the servant he met considers me as such. Father is so confused these days that most of the servants and villagers come to me for instruction. I am afraid that we keep him in his quarters as much as possible as he will wander into the woods and then follow the river down to the bridge and knock on the hermitage door or run across the bridge. It is most undignified and I am glad that our mother is no longer alive to witness it. The healers and doctors have told us that he is a victim of old age and will never get better. Come if you wish, but rushing will make no difference. We are looking after him and I am taking more duties from him.

Lord Baldwin of Pridias

Brother,

Thank you for the letter. I was rather hoping to hear from Father and am hoping that signing your letter to me as Lord Baldwin was a mistake. I am your brother and not your servant. I will come and visit and make sure everything is alright. I expect you have managed to take over control of the family money and I would like to speak to Reginald about that. I have seen evidence of spirits on our land and I am proud of our lineage - apparently, you are not.

Sir Geoffrey of Orcherton

Geoffrey,

I hope this letter reaches you safely. The messenger
is my most trusted servant. Sad to say, there are few
here at Pridias Hall I can trust. All these years I have
ruled them well and they now obey your brother
rather than me. I am neither senile nor suffering
from mental decay and yet I am kept under lock and
key in the south tower at the Hall while Baldwin
swaggers about spending our money on himself
rather than our estates and there is a danger our
people could starve. The lady I speak to is a Priestess
of ancient times. I am not hallucinating nor making
this up. She is an immortal soul who knew Tristan
and Iseult and King Mark and all our ancestors. I first
saw her at Golant standing at the water's edge with
her pale blue dress floating on the tide and her long
pale red hair blowing behind her. I thought she was
the most beautiful creature I have ever seen. Even
more than your mother and she was very lovely as
you know. I say creature because she was
otherworldly – is otherworldly and has become my
confidante. I used to love talking to you about the
old ways and the family secrets and the magic and
since you left us to take over those lands at Devon
which I still want to visit, I have no ally here. The
Priestess has told me such stories and explained the
mysteries of the world to me. I would like to pass
them on to you, but not by message. I will tell you
when you come and come you must. Your brother
has taken hold of the purse strings and is keeping my
friends away, telling them that I am too ill to be
seen. I have a spare key which he does not know
about and let myself out and ride to Golant when I

can. The guards at the bridge allow me across and I believe that I have their silence.

Richard, your father.

Reginald,

I have been receiving strange correspondence from Father and Baldwin and wonder if you have the time to travel from Truro to Pridias and find out what is going on. Father tells me he is being locked in his room and Baldwin tells me Father is incapable of running the estates and has taken control of the money. If necessary I shall travel down from Orcherton, but am in the middle of some deals involving my own estates and may well be going into politics. Do let me know as soon as you can and tread carefully with Baldwin, we both know what he is like. The family send their love.

Geoffrey and Isabella

Geoffrey and Isabella,

I am at Pridias, having left Truro directly after I received you message. You worried me and in some ways, you were quite correct so to do. Father is definitely not as he was, rambling constantly about ghost women, well one woman, some priestess he believes that she is. I suspect it is all in his imagination. Unless it is a village woman trying to obtain money or worse – a marriage proposal. That would upset Baldwin I have no doubt. I asked Father's attendants and they believe that he is suffering from brain inflammation, some sort of delayed shock reaction following Mother's death. I am currently waiting for the doctor to arrive as I write and see what he says. Father says that he has nothing more to tell me, but wishes I would remain at the Hall. I explained that I have my own life to live and that he must rely on the good graces of Baldwin and his family. He is to inherit after all and you and I must make our own way. I have told Baldwin that he has no legal right to take over the finances, although from what I have seen so far, I don't think he is doing anything rash. He is neither a drinker nor a gambler and wishes to keep the estate together, so there is scant reason for him to gamble with his own inheritance. You and Isabella will be made welcome here, I have no doubt. I shall come to Orcherton soon in order that I can through the leases and properties for you and Isabella. I am cheaper and more reliable than any of those Devon men!

Best wishes to my nephews.

Reginald

My dear interfering Sir Geoffrey,

How dare you send for Reginald and ask him to investigate the way I am running estates here at

Pridias? Hoping to have me convicted of some form of fraud and then you two can inherit instead of me? Well, he couldn't find anything wrong and my doctor has confirmed that Father is suffering from senile decay and that it is a good job I have taken more control as the estate could fail and the people starve under his command. The Prior has also expressed concern at Father's ramblings. He is worried about income to the Priory and the upkeep of the bridge and success of the harvests. I am more than capable of taking care of that. If you were here on a regular basis you would see that Father is old and sick, but you are not. You are in your secure Devon estates with a rich wife and plenty of money. I must say that you are no longer welcome here at Pridias until I receive a full apology and acknowledgment that Father is sick and I am in no way caring for him incorrectly.

Baldwin, Lord of Pridias.

Baldwin,

I don't know why you are making such a fuss. I worry about my Father and Reginald lives nearer and was able to call and see him easier than I. I shall call whenever I wish, the estate is still under Father's name and as a Pridias you cannot ban me nor my family. I don't think our ancestors would approve, do you? Now, let us behave like gentlemen and not argue. I would be greatly obliged if you could keep me informed as to his health.

Geoffrey

Father,

I have heard back from Reginald about his visit and
he tells me that you are quite well, but fears that
there is a woman who is trying to bewitch you. I am
sure that this is nonsense and I am quite willing to
believe in your Priestess. What is it that she requires
of you? I agree that there are supernatural forces at
work everywhere in our world and I have many
memories of the stories you told us of the woodland
spirits and the Disbobmajig who lives under the
bridge. You told us of Jehanne and Tristen and their
magical ability to keep the Pridias land under our
control and I have believed you despite never seeing
any evidence myself. Baldwin is telling me that I am
banned from seeing you and coming home but I am
paying no attention to that stupidity. Shall I come?

Best love Geoffrey

My dearest son,

I am so pleased to hear from you. Reginald did come,
but seemed to spend more time arguing with
Baldwin about who was right about the finances. I

am sad that none of my boys have the same love for this magical and special place that your ancestors did. Our ancestors lived and ruled here before the Saxons and the Romans and can be traced back to Lyonesse and they all loved and protected these lands. The Priestess tells me that a spell has been cast over my children and I must do my best to break it. The Disperkel and other spirits cannot protect us when we do not acknowledge their existence. Nothing can exist if denied. Nothing. She has taught me a lot. I speak to her on many occasions, but shall not tell you how, as you may tell your brothers and they will stop that avenue of escape if they can. I hope the family are well and I would visit your Devon lands if the Priestess did not advise against it.

Your only father

Richard

My dear wife,

I hope you are having an excellent visit with your sister and have to tell you that I miss you very much. The boys play with their friends and are very well and happy and you must not worry about them. I hope that our brother-in-law will return to health soon and I understand that you must take care of your sister during her troubles. I want to ask your advice on the ongoing saga of our father Richard. I do not know who to believe, my brothers or my Father. Both seem very set on their side of the story. I do not know if this Priestess is a conniving woman, a figment of his imagination or worse – a real phantom! Perhaps when you have returned, I shall visit him. You may come too and the boys are excited at the thought of a visit there. I should hate Father to die when I haven't said goodbye and I have to admit only to you, my dearest Isabella, that I am concerned about Baldwin and his actions in spite of his statements to the contrary. Please do keep yourself well and do not overtire yourself looking after others. We both know what you are like.

Your loving husband Joffrey

Husband,

I am quite well and am taking quite as much rest as I need. My thought is that you and the boys must go to Pridias immediately and see what is happening. Perhaps do not announce your arrival. And my dearest dear – we both know that there are many unusual happenings in this world. My father often spoke of the people who live under the sea and his father would speak of men and women who knew magic and my family do not lie. Go to Pridias and write from there. My best love.

Isabella

Isabella,

We are at Pridias and I have to say that our welcome was unusual. Baldwin had instructed the guards at the bridge to not allow us through. Can you believe it? The guards obeyed his orders and then went back into their towers while (accidentally) leaving the bridge gates opened. I stopped at Golant on the way to Baldwin's Bridge and I must say that I had almost forgotten how beautiful it is there. The little church and the small harbour with the colourful fishing boats moored on the jetty were imaged in paintings by Mother. I must find those again, I think they were put in one of the towers. The cottagers, mainly fishing people, seemed surprised to see us but pleased nonetheless. I asked about Father and they said they often see him. He rides there and sits on the jetty and looks over the water and talks to himself, they told me. There was no hermit nor monk at the chapel and I do believe the door was locked. I could not gain access anyway. By the time, we arrived at the Hall, we were very tired and I was in no mood for an argument. Baldwin's servants answered the door and told me to wait! Eventually Baldwin arrived and told me that I should have informed him of my visit. I am afraid I told a lie and said that I had sent a message which he obviously hadn't received. We were allowed in and he passed off the original entry refusal and said that we were welcome and asked most prettily after your welfare. His wife has become very fat since we last saw her and I do not believe that she is with child again, but I did not ask. She was also very miserable and appeared angry that we were here. They do have full residence as Lord and Lady with nothing in view that shows Father is still alive. We ate and drank well and were not able to see Father before we retired. However, in the night he appeared in my quarters and I was shocked to see how much he had aged. He would not tell me how he got to my room without the servants stopping him, but his tale was worth listening to. I must begin by saying that he did not seem mentally unwell, just anxious and over excited. He told me that the Priestess is related to Jehanne and has the interests of the Pridias lands at heart. I asked if I could meet her and he said yes, to my astonishment. And meet her I did! The boys were asked to come but only Roger wanted to as Piers had arranged to go sailing with Baldwin and Baldwin assumed that we were only exploring the woods. He let Father come with us and we went to the woods north of Luxulyan. Father rode as though he was meeting his maker and we struggled to keep up. In a clearing, which I swear I have never seen before, was a hut built from stone with an oak roof. In some ways, the building was very similar to the hermitage by Baldwin's Bridge. There was a white horse who roamed freely and wolves, white and blue wolves, reminiscent of the wolves our ancestors kept as guardians. I don't know why we let the habit go, they are beautiful beasts. Father jumped from his horse and ran into the little cottage and then came out followed by the most ethereal woman I have ever seen. You are beautiful my love, but she! There was a rainbowed aura surrounding her. She wore pale blue with a white over tunic. Her hair was blonde-red and flowed free and was long and jewelled. She opened her arms to us in welcome and we dismounted and went to her and bowed. She took us to a table which sat under an ancient oak tree and was laden with food. We sat and talked for hours and I don't think that I can remember a small portion of what was said. What I do know is that Baldwin has been bewitched by his wife's family who want the lands for their own. They want Richard dead and then they will work on Baldwin and then claim the lands. She told us how it can be stopped and yet I cannot remember what she said. There was just a feeling that we had somehow agreed the right thing to do. As we rode away I was convinced that the family was to be saved and Father was happier than before. When we arrived back at the Hall, Baldwin and his wife were very upset and had the servants take Father directly to his rooms. We are to stay for two more days and I shall write again.

My deepest love Joffrey

My dear sister Isabella,

I write to let you know that your husband and sons are sick with fever here at Pridias. Our dear Father is ill too. They are in my own Hall at Landreath and are in the good hands of my servants there. We do not want the children infected and so for now we shall keep apart. They are not in danger and so you must not worry. You must not attend them if you are to keep yourself well.

Your loving brother
Baldwin, Lord of Pridias

Joffrey,

This letter is short as it is my third and I have received no reply from you or Baldwin. I am very worried, please write to me. I am returned to Orcherton and will send soldiers if I hear nothing soon.

Isabella

Mother,

I have escaped the Hall and am at the hermitage - safe. The Priestess helped me and left me here. We were to go the Priory, but that is not now deemed safe. Father and Grandfather are locked in the tower at Pridias, but we have set in motion a plan to free them. She knows spells and soon they will be free.

Roger

My dear wife,

We are all free! Your soldiers arrived as the Priestess cast the spell. It was a binding spell and the soldiers – the mercenary soldiers of Baldwin - were killed. They all had a sudden fever and became paralysed for long enough for us to be freed. The Priestess was magnificent as she opened her arms, this time not in welcome but with power. She grew Isabella! To the size of a giant! We were all free and Father was as happy as he ever has been. Baldwin fainted and did not recover consciousness for two days. His wife immediately died of the fever (she was just fat and not with child) and the Priestess said that Pridias is now free and her work is done. It was so wonderful my love. Roger and I shall be back at Orcherton soon. I am sending the soldiers back with Piers and this letter and a few items which have been given to me by my Father. (Including Mother's paintings – aren't they wonderful?) Baldwin now accepts that he has been under the curse of his wife and her devilish family and the Prior and the monks have been here to cleanse the Halls and the lands. Reginald is ensuring that legal safeguards are in place and Baldwin has given the Priory a little land to sweeten their resolve towards our family.

Our best love to you.

Joffrey and Roger.

My Dear Geoffrey,

I know I thanked you when you were here, but I want to again. To have the lands restored as they were and my heir Baldwin back within the fold and no longer under the influence of that dreadful wife of his, is heaven to me. Priestess is with me less often but I can still call at her cottage in the woods. Although I do admit that I am not always able to find it. She did tell us though that there are many versions of our world existing alongside each other and we can choose which one in which to reside at any moment. Do you remember? There is so much that she told us and I think I must write it down and hide it somewhere. I do know that if I say any of this publicly, the Prior will tell the Bishop and he will tell the Earl and I do also know that Reginald will suddenly become more Church than Pridias and judge me badly. I have revived the walled garden. I have planted lavender, roses, all the herbs and medicinal plants and trees. The colours and scents are marvellous and renewing. On some days, I ride to the old fort which was at one time King Mark's Palace and watch the monks working with the broom and indigo and rubia and woad. I wanted to reclaim Carnubelbanathel between that castle and Golant, but it is still leased to the Priory as agreed by our Pridias ancestors and Baldwin wants to honour the contract. The monks are very skilled and have helped me re-establish the garden. They have grown so many plants at the Priory and purchase cuttings and seedlings from the merchants when they arrive by sea. When I am finally gone to our ancestors, I ask that many of my flowers are on display at the chapel. Yes, I shall write about the truths she told us, such a different interpretation of the Christian teachings. This Rome looks after itself and has put ridiculously costumed nincompoops between man and God. Man can find salvation without the Church but there is no money, power nor control in that truth. Rome will never let the truth be told. I shall hide the writings where you alone know they can be found. The weather has been glorious here recently, the woods and meadows and beach and sea are so wonderful. These lands have always been and will always be Pridias lands.

Your loving father Richard.

My dear Roger,

I found them. I found the writings and I shall return with them and we shall hide them. Baldwin and Reginald will never know, for I fear that neither of my brothers will carry on any of the old ways. Now that my beloved father is laid to rest in our chapel and Baldwin has remarried a very religious woman and if the writings were to be discovered, they will be destroyed. I went to the cottage of the Priestess and she told me that she is leaving now to join Richard and our ancestors. She prophecies a time when the Pridias lands will be far from the sea and the Priory will crumble. She says the remaining lands will remain in Pridias hands for hundreds of years and then into other hands for 280 years until they are recovered by a blood Pridias. Then the spirits and witches and guardians will return. The Priestess will return then too. You will be part of this secret Roger, as will your son and his son and so on. I went to the walled garden and sat for many hours where I meditated and heard Father speak to me. He is happy and I am happy. I shall be home soon my boy.

Your loving father.

Geoffrey.

I AM RICH

Featuring Geoffrey de Pridias

(1200 – 1270)

"That is a wonderful painting Baldwin. I assume it is of our Priestess as it captures her likeness so, but who painted it?"

"Our latest monk at the hermitage chapel. He was in her presence before Father died."

"The setting is the clearing I see," said Geoffrey.

"It is, have you had time to visit it yet?"

"No, but I shall. When we were here for the funeral, there was no time for visiting with all the arrangements and the grief."

"And your need to be alone with your new and very young bride!"

"Nicholaa would never take me away from my family!"

"Calm yourself Geoffrey! I jest only! She is a beautiful young woman and I am pleased, as is our brother Reginald to have such a lovely sister. The match has helped us greatly here at Pridias."

"Because her father has such political connections? It is a good job, as she brought no money to the match," said Geoffrey.

"But she did bring a 20-year-old body to it!"

"Your new wife is not much older Baldwin!"

"I know. Isn't it amazing that these young women and their fathers find eligible and filthy- rich, titled, old men attractive?"

"It is a mystery!"

"Your boys are married now Geoffrey. We are getting old."

"It seems ridiculous that Roger has two children and another on the way and even Piers is now expecting. I am still playing on the Pridias beach and sailing out to sea with old John in my mind."

"John, he was a kind old man. You know his grandson now lives in his old cottage? He doesn't fish, he is frightened of the sea he says, but he helped Father with the garden."

"You will keep the garden? Father was so proud of it."

"Of course and it will be tended as lovingly as when he was here. I feel as though he is still there, perhaps all our people are there and not in the crypt. It would be nice to think so."

Baldwin took another drink of wine. The brothers were eating and drinking in the dining hall. The furniture in this room had changed little in over a hundred years. The table, chairs and side tables were all English oak. The tapestries and paintings were exquisite and ancient and kept in first class condition by the servants. The candlesticks and plate were gold and silver and the carpets woven and embroidered in silk and wool. Many of the decorations and trinkets had been bought from foreign merchants over the years. The glassware, expensive and gold rimmed, reflected the candlelight. Here, they had hosted many banquets sealing marriage and business deals.

"I know that you are going away tomorrow and I wish to ask a favour Baldwin."

"Anything Geoffrey."

"I would like to remain at Pridias Hall in your absence and remember the time I was a child. I am fifty-one years old and may never have the chance to amuse myself in my old home in this way again."

"And yet you and all of your family will always be welcome here."

"I know and I am grateful, but..."

"Of course, Geoffrey, I think I understand. Yes, yes. We shall be at St Ives for one week and you may stay for the entire time and beyond if it, if you desire. I shall instruct the servants and the soldiers of this and you, my brother shall be free of any interference."

When Geoffrey came down the following morning, Baldwin and his family had already left. The maidservant brought his breakfast into the dining room and dropped an embarrassed curtsey as she did so. Geoffrey ate leisurely before he went out to the walls and looked out to sea. The tide was coming in and appeared to be bringing a storm with it. The boats bobbed and tacked on the waves, hoping to make safe harbour before the storm landed. He saw the herdsmen ushering their stock towards shelter and had an urge to help them. He was a young boy, free to run about the estates. He laughed to himself in the memory.

He hadn't lied to Baldwin, he wanted the time at Pridias alone. He owned and ruled huge estates in Devon but Pridias was home. He was also glad to be free of his young wife for a time. She was relentless in her nagging about – everything. Her desire for a child and her desire for jewellery and clothes was insatiable and she literally never shut up. It had seemed such a good idea to marry a beautiful young woman, but it became exhausting after only a few months.

Geoffrey had yesterday sent her a letter saying that it was imperative he remain at Pridias for the time being and he would return shortly. What Geoffrey really wanted, was to find the writings of his father. Richard had told him by letter during those final years that he would write down all the spiritual and magical teachings he had learned from the lips of the

Priestess. He had said that he would hide it in a place that only Geoffrey could find and despite many hours of thought, Geoffrey could not remember any such place. He decided that he would search the estates until he found the prize. Geoffrey hoped that being home would prompt his memory and being alone would deter questions from his brothers.

He decided that he would clear the ground beneath his feet first and that meant checking the Hall and then the garden, followed by the grounds. If no luck there, he must spread his search to the clearing and the hermitage and bridge and then perhaps Golant and the rest of the estate. Suddenly he recognised the enormity of such a task to be undertaken by one man. He would have to rethink. He went outside and walked to the cliff edge. His first intention was to go to the beach until he saw that the tide was coming in and would soon cut off his exit. So, he trudged further south until he arrived at the Pridias chapel.

So recently he has been here with his wife, sons and their families joining the line of surviving Pridias and their soldiers and servants behind the body of his father. The sun had been streaming across the land that day and the light wind had been strong enough to move the many flags and banners which depicted the Pridias colours. The garlands of flowers which lined the route had come not only from the Hall gardens, but from the cottages and farmers and the Priory and other Manors. Not one bouquet or offering had come under duress, everyone wanted to honour Richard, Lord of Pridias Manor. What a day that had been, there had been as much joy as sorrow. Geoffrey wished that Isabella had been by his side rather than the beautiful and self-absorbed Nicholaa.

Isabella was such a Lady in all senses and he still had not got over the shock of her sudden death. She died on her seat at Orcherton overlooking the estuary and the sea. The doctor told them all that it was a quick end and that her heart had given out. Geoffrey soon married Nicholaa for two reasons, one, he thought she might be a younger version of Isabella and two, it was supposed to be a good political connection for his family and his own political ambitions. It hadn't quite worked out like that and now he missed Isabella more than ever.

He opened the chapel door and entered just as the storm arrived and slammed the door closed behind him. The change in pressure blew out some of the candles and left most of the chapel in darkness.

"Hello!" he called out. "Anyone here?"

There was no answer and Geoffrey walked to the altar. He picked up a taper and began lighting the candles, all of which seemed determined to blow out as quickly as they were lit. He turned around quickly when he heard the main door open again, but it was closed.

"Hello?" he asked.

Apart from a shuffling sound which Geoffrey decided to put down to the blowing wind, there was no one else in the chapel with him. So, why did he feel so anxious, with goose pimples all over his body?

The extra candle light shone into a few corners and Geoffrey's spirits lifted. He moved about the chapel, lifting this and looking in that, wondering where the documents could be. Or was it in the form of a book? He knew that the monks could do that but surely, they would have been alarmed at the content? Unless Richard had paid the monk well, they always liked money. But, there was nothing to be found up here and he knew he must go down to the crypt. He lit a torch and opened the door at the top of the stairs. A musty and decaying smell hit his nostrils which he knew would clear the longer the door was open. As he took the top step, the last thing he saw from the chapel was a flash of lightning and he heard the sound of thunder and wind. It almost put him off descending, instead he shook the feeling and walked quickly down to the crypt.

Once down there, he wondered what on earth he had been thinking. His hands shook as he tried to use his taper to light the large candles on the sconces and candle stands. They wouldn't light immediately and he stopped himself from looking behind or at any corner of the crypt when he heard a scuffle or a whisper.

"I am too old to be in here on my own," he said.

Even being surrounded by all his family could not help his anxious feeling. There was an almost overpowering smell of decomposition and he made a mental note to call back the stonemason who clearly had done a poor job of sealing his father's tomb.

"I am rich," said a voice.

"So am I!" answered Geoffrey, chuckling at his witticism and trying not to become hysterical.

The dust on the stone floor swirled and Geoffrey felt a cold breeze about his body. He tried to ignore it, instead busying himself by looking amongst the coffins for the notes. He was finding nothing except butterflies in his stomach and a desire to evacuate his bladder. He had no intention to do that in this place, not unless he were to be locked in for any reason. That thought was enough to make him trot up the steps to the door. He lifted the latch and pushed, but there was resistance. Geoffrey's heart almost stopped as he pulled and pushed. He was sure there was something behind him, watching him.

"I am rich," something said and Geoffrey wondered why a demon would want to brag in such a way.

He remembered to lift the latch and was soon in the chapel and he immediately thought about the candles he had left lighted down below. He decided that he would wander about the chapel a little longer and regain Lordly composure, before he went down to blow them out. The storm was now at its height and the electric tension could be felt in the chapel. As the lightning flashed, Geoffrey went to the stained-glass window to look out. If there was anyone there, he could not see them. The rain was so heavy and the sky so dark, that an army could be marching past and be invisible. The constant thunder and lightning indicated that the storm was overhead and Geoffrey knew he would be stupid to leave the chapel now.

At least he had more time to search here. He sat on one of the solid oak benches and stared at the altar. This was distinctly Christian, with a crucifix, incense and prayer books. Geoffrey knew that this had been done for the benefit of the Priory and the increasingly conformative neighbours. He knew that in the oak chest in the small room behind the altar lay some personalised Pridias items for – he should say worship, but perhaps magic would be more appropriate. On the walls were several likenesses of his ancestors, the Lords anyway, made from their death masks. The women were represented on wall paintings and each of them looked beautiful. He thought about the Lords prior to Richard, the father of Paganus who were not immortalised here, but elsewhere under quoits on the estates. He also realised that there would never be a death mask of him or his sons in this crypt. Baldwin and his descendants would be represented here. He felt disappointed and decided there and then that he would have a crypt built at Orcherton. He would keep it separate to the Orcherton tombs for purity, he thought. Even though he was now the owner of hundreds of acres of Devon lands and many Devon properties, Geoffrey considered himself firmly Cornish. And a Pridias. He wondered if his descendants would feel the same.

An almighty crack of thunder made him jump up and look around just as the front door swung open with a gust of wind. He ran to it and looked out. There was no chance of him leaving just yet. His view was still obliterated by the rain, but he had a few glimpses of the huge waves and he said a silent prayer for anyone caught at sea or on land in this frightening weather. He was glad that he had not brought his horse as he would have been sorely tempted to bring him into the chapel for shelter.

"I am rich," came the voice.

"Who is this?" asked Geoffrey and the statement was repeated. This time he was sure that the voice had come from the crypt. He was going to have to go and check.

He put a large candle into the hurricane lamp he found by the door and made sure that it was securely fastened. He put two candles in his tunic pocket and two tapers. As an afterthought, he unsheathed his dagger. He mused that he did not prepare this much for a hunt. He opened the crypt door and jammed it open with one of the oak benches. The smell hit him again and he put his hand to his mouth, almost cutting his nose with the dagger. The lights from downstairs flickered and he knew he must go and blow them out if he did not want to remove all evidence of his forebears in one giant explosion.

Geoffrey was so nervous that he could scarcely keep his balance as he stepped down into the crypt. He pondered that he should only feel secure when his lamp lit the corners of the room, as if that made it alright. He reached the far end of the crypt where the candles were and blew them out. His hurricane lamp left enough light to see by – until it went out and the crypt door slammed shut. He guessed the outside chapel door had blown open again.

"I am rich."

"Who are you? If you are trying to scare me, you are doing a great job."

Well that should get the spirits properly rattled, Geoffrey thought. The smell was becoming stronger and he found that he was breathless, whether with fear or decay he could not say. Each breath took three short attempts to come in and he couldn't work out how he was breathing out. He put his hand behind him and felt around the candles and their holders hoping for a flint or some way of lighting the candles. He did not turn around, fearing being grabbed or poked or being touched. He managed to control his breathing a little better and tried to listen. If he was to be murdered by a demon of some sort at least he wanted a chance of knowing when it would occur.

He could hear nothing and so shuffled forward through the thick darkness with one hand moving across the tombs at the side of the crypt so that he could be sure he was heading towards the stairs. The tombs felt cool and the mortar flaked against his hand and Geoffrey hoped that he would not accidentally pull out a stone or knock off a lid. Blood relatives they may be - but hell no.

He could smell that the strongest scent came from the end tomb, which he knew was that of his father.

"I am rich."

Geoffrey was sure that the sound was next to his ear. Could it be coming from a tomb?

"Hello?"

He had responded too many times now and not had a reply, so he vowed not to answer again. Instead he walked forward, eager to get out and determined not to be side-tracked. He quickened his step as he guessed he must be almost at the bottom step by now. He walked in an exaggerated way hoping that his foot would soon touch the raised stone which represented his escape.

"Ooooo!" he squealed as he felt something move down his neck. He put his hand up to his hairline and turned around and moved his arm from side to side and thankfully contacted nothing but the wall and tombs.

Oh no! He heard the sliding of stone against stone followed by rocks landing on the floor. The smell was stronger now and he thought he heard someone trying to get out of a tomb. He stopped breathing when he heard someone or something, jump down on the floor.

"I am rich," it said.

"Not sure that you are sir," Geoffrey said. "If you are a demon, then you are not rich, are you?"

Geoffrey heard more creaking and crumbling and the sliding and crunching of stone against stone. He hoped against forlorn hope that this did not signal more demons climbing out of their tombs. With each sliding there came a renewed smell of decay. The sound of feet hitting the floor and hands against the walls made his heart beat too fast and then stop as it if it was trying to regulate itself. The atmosphere was thick with the smell and the shrinking space inside the crypt and Geoffrey thought that he might be dying right here, right now. This must be how it felt. The Roman Church had promised that the process of death was to be a horrendous experience and one which every sinner deserved.

No, not me.

"What is this?" he shouted and as he did he felt his power rise within him again. If he was dying, he was going down fighting.

"This is my life and my eternity!" he said fiercely. "Stop trying to frighten me. I say again, who are you?"

"I am rich."

"I am rich." Another voice.

"I am rich." And another.

Geoffrey said, "Stop!"

"I am rich." A fourth voice.

"I am Pagan."

"I am Baldwin."

"I am Nicholas."

Geoffrey fell to his knees and began to cry.

"So, I am dead?"

"No, my son. You came here to find the teachings and I have been trying to tell you where they are."

As he spoke, the dark in the crypt brightened a little and Geoffrey could see the pale silver features of his ancestors smiling and nodding behind his father.

"Where are the teachings? And are you all alright?"

"Haha! I see where your priorities lie Geoffrey! The documents are in my tomb, I asked your brother to bury the container with me and I knew it would be safe there until you came alone. Just reach in, it won't be too sticky!"

"We are all quite well, my darling." It was Morgana and she looked as she had when Geoffrey last saw her. She was cloaked in a misty blue and white haze and reminded Geoffrey of the descriptions of ghosts he had heard over the years. So, it was true.

"I am not ready to join you," he said.

"No, no, no my boy. You have a lot to do yet. You will be quite an old man before you join us but don't despair! It's really nice there! Quickly now!"

Geoffrey reached in and felt around the tomb. The light from his long dead, glowing and amiable ancestors assisted his search and soon his hand rested against a gold cylinder. He took it out and held it to his chest. There was a round of applause which Geoffrey considered unusual but accepted nonetheless.

"Goodnight, sleep tight, Joffrey," said Morgana.

"Don't rush to join us yet," added his father and began to climb back into his tomb. Geoffrey watched as each ancestor, male and female returned to their stone coffins and slid their lids back. As they did so, the dark crept in a little more with each closure until Geoffrey stood in the dark, all alone. This time he was not afraid and he wondered if he ever would be again.

"My Lord!"

The crypt door had opened and a servant with a lantern stood at the top of the stairs.

"Yes John, I am here."

"Oh, my Lord! We were so worried about you with this storm and all. We have been looking for you. Were you locked in?"

"No, John. I am quite safe. I was just visiting the family."

"Of course, my Lord, only it has been such a long time and supper has long been ready at the Hall."

Geoffrey walked upstairs and saw that it was dark outside. They left together out of the chapel door and Geoffrey noticed that the weather was calm and warm and the sea peaceful.

"Were you not frightened in the dark all alone, my Lord?" asked John with genuine concern.

"Not at all John. They are my family after all."

John nodded but did not seem convinced. He had been frightened enough just searching for his master.

Geoffrey enjoyed the return walk along the coast path and looked from the view across the bay to the twinkling lights of Tywardreath and the Priory and back to the dark shadow of the walled Pridias Hall atop of which hung bright flaming lanterns to mark their destination.

The following day he went to the clearing and met with the Priestess for one last time. Following the meeting he wrote to his son.

My dear Roger,

I found them. I found the writings and I shall return with them and we shall hide them. Baldwin and Reginald will never know, for I fear that neither of my brothers will carry on any of the old ways. Now that my beloved father is laid to rest in our chapel and Baldwin has remarried a very religious woman, if the writings were to be discovered, they will be destroyed. I went to the cottage of the Priestess and she told me that she is leaving now to join Richard and our ancestors. She prophecies a time when the Pridias lands will be far from the sea and the Priory will crumble. She says the remaining lands will remain in Pridias hands for hundreds of years and then into other hands for 280 years until they are recovered by a blood Pridias. Then the spirits and witches and guardians will return. The Priestess will return then too. You will be part of this secret Roger, as will your son and his son and so on. I went to the walled garden and sat for many hours where I meditated and heard Father speak to me. He is happy and I am happy. I shall be home soon my boy.

Your loving father.

Geoffrey.